The Bridge To Forever

A Perry Normal Adventure

Mason Stone

To my Pig, my forever. And to my Auntie Jean, who believed in me when I needed it most.

Disclaimer

Stay in touch with Mason at:
http://perryisnormal.blogspot.ca

Order his books at myredpine@gmail.com

CONTENTS

ACT I   WHEN DARKNESS FALLS

CHAPTER ONE   HOME SWEET HOME

Perry Normal was an ordinary boy who seemed to have extraordinary experiences. He didn't ask for them. He didn't expect his life would be anything different from what his family or friends experienced, living in a small town in upstate New York.

As much as he tried to be a part of his community, and his school, somehow Destiny kept him from ever having a regular, predictable existence.

He was special. He had no idea why.

Every day the kids went to school, and every night they came home, ate dinner, and did their homework – while quietly texting each other, sharing secrets, and bemoaning their fate as Seventh Graders.

And like most people, Perry was close to his family: his Mom, who was a school board administrator, his Dad who was a financial analyst, his sister Gabrielle, who was a bit older and was a pain in the neck when she wanted to be.

He was especially close to his Grandma and Grandpa on his mother's side. He adored them, and the feeling was mutual. Perry spent summer holidays on their farm, just enjoying being eleven years old, and doing whatever he felt like doing.

More than anything, Perry wanted to be a scientist, a real scientist. He wanted to major in Astronomy, or something closely related to it, and go to a good university to learn how to do proper research, and apply the fundamental reasoning that good science is known for.

He was already the Science champion at Brackendale Middle School. He got straight 'A's, he won first prize in last Fall's state-wide Science Fair. He informally tutors his friends in Science and Math. Everybody values Perry's presence, even the Science teacher Mr. Matson.

"Curiosity killed the cat, I'm tellin' you I know where it's at," crooned the band on the radio. Perry was curious, and good science is about being curious and asking the right questions.

Last year, Perry asked Mr. Matson about the nature of Time, and whether time travel was possible. Such thinking leads to new adventures, as Perry found out!

Perry's older sister who would go into 10th grade soon, and Perry adored her, although he would never ever admit it. Gabrielle liked to pick on him which, when you think about it, means she cares a lot about her little brother in a funny way that only siblings really understand.

His parents were hard-working, decent American folks, who tried to give their kids the best things in life: a nice home, nice clothes, summer camp and other essential experiences for American kids.

They had a pretty good relationship with both Gabby and Perry. Nothing was held back; they could communicate openly about just about anything. They were open-minded, which set a good example, for Perry tended to be a little narrow-minded about the way the world worked, and what the laws of the Universe were.

He was totally invested in The Scientific Method, and truly believed that Science and Reason could explain all the phenomena that humans could ever experience. Period.

A typical schoolday for Perry looked like this:

7:30 a.m.   Get up, shower, get dressed, go downstairs for breakfast.

8:15 a.m.   Get his backpack and lunch, and walk fifteen minutes to Isaac Newton Blvd. to Brackendale Middle School.

8:45 a.m.   Put his stuff in his locker, greet his friends(aka 'The Gang'), go to 1st Period class.

10:15 a.m.   Go to 2nd Period. Maybe grab a snack from his locker, or the Caf if there was time.

11:30 a.m.   Finish class, and go for lunch. Hang out with Henry, Max, Robert, etc. Maybe go to the Library to find some information for an assignment.

1:00 p.m.   Back for 3rd Period. Try to stay awake like everyone else did, cause they all probably stayed up late playing games, reading, chatting online or on their cell. Late night was social media time. After parents went to bed.

2:15 p.m.	Last Period. If your timetable was half-decent, it would *not* be Math with Mr. Kruschevsky, (nicknamed 'Crusher'). That would kill. By 4th Period, your brain was fried from too much thinking, remembering, calculating stuff.
3:30 p.m.	Release from the dungeon of rules, classes, in-class presentations (that were supremely annoying), and much more. In short, FREEDOM!!

Where the gang went after school was a local institution: The Malt Shop. 'Serving customers quality meals since 1958' said the green and white sign outside. This was the center of social life for kids at Brackendale Middle School.

The big attraction, apart from the tasty food that kids really go for, was meeting your friends, and being a part of the people who made your day-to-day life tolerable, or even fun.

"Did you see Miss Latimer's ring? It's a diamond!"

Rita and Margot and Katya were gushing and gossiping like crazy about the Socials teacher who arrived last year from Toronto.

Everybody got that Canadians were not much different from Americans; we watched the same TV shows, ate burgers and fries, love baseball and basketball, and valued their high standard of living and democratic freedoms just as much as we do.

The weather is no different in upper New York State than it is in Ontario and Quebec. They speak French in Quebec, which is kind of cool. Mrs. Latimer said she had to study it in tenth grade.

"I didn't know she had a boyfriend!" chirped Charmaine.

"Who would want to be her BF?" Max said. "She probably makes him mark her History and Geography assignments."

"Yeah. Can you imagine how boring getting married to a teacher would be?" Now Robert weighed in.

"Mr. Matson is married," Rita said.

"Yeah, to another teacher!" Robert said.

"Food is here," said Henry, adjusting his fries with a fork, so that the yummy gravy uniformly covered each one; then he began to eat each solitary potato piece with serious attention.

Henry Schuyler was Perry's best friend. He was a total science geek. He read nothing but Science Fiction novels, or scientific journals and magazines. His room at home was littered with <u>Scientific American</u>, <u>Nature</u>, <u>Popular Science</u>, and physical remnants of his own personal experiments: chemistry apparatus like beakers and test tubes full of chemical residue from failed explosions, cardboard boxes with leaves and stems of various edible wild plants that grow in the area, even a cat skeleton he found in the bushes.

He had a mineral collection that included a piece of the Canyon Diablo Meteorite from Arizona. He also had a hamster in a cage which ran on its little wheel ceaselessly. Henry called him Orville, after the famous Wright Brother, and Father of Aviation.

"Yo, people! Anybody heard the news about Grant? His house burned down on the weekend."

Everyone put down their glass and stared at Mike.

Mike did not usually speak to Perry's gang because he was part of his own tough-guy crowd at school, the boys who smoked, and probably smoked weed, and gave teachers and students they didn't like a hard time. Randy the Gorilla was his best friend. Randy had attitude. Their whole bunch had attitude.

"Yeah, it was on the news. So I talked to Grant personally." You could see Mike was proud of his investigative journalist skills.

"He said his old man fell asleep on the couch with a cigarette in his hand. Probably passed out dead drunk. At least, that's what I think.

Anyhow, couch caught fire, set the walls and ceiling on fire. Scared the shit out of everyone, but they all got out okay. House was totaled. Grant showed me. A black shell was all that was left of the downstairs. Grant got most of his stuff out ok, so that was good."

"Where's he going to live?" said Rita and Charmaine, at the same time.

"His uncle will take them in. He's in Fernville, so Grant maybe has to finish the year over at their school. Not as good as *our* school, of course. But hey! Shit happens!"

No one said much more about it. Deep down, everyone felt that if something happens to one of them, it happens to all of them. Like the U.S. Marine Corps Code. All for one and one for all. Or something.

So they switched back to gossip; who was interested in whom, which teachers were easy markers, which courses next year were bird courses that anyone could pass, and so on.

Life was good in Brackendale. It was a real community. They had a community center with after-school activities like sports for kids, and bridge and bingo for seniors.

There was virtually no crime in Brackendale. What little there was related to petty theft or vandalism, certainly no big-city style violent crime. Girls could be out late and not worry.

That made parents like Perry's feel really good about living in a small town.

They didn't own a gun. They looked after the neighbor's cat when the folks next door, or across the street, went on vacation. That's the kind of town it was.

***

Perry's mother's parents lived not far from town on about ten acres of rich farmland with good soil. They had immigrated from Italy after the Second

World War ended in 1945, and Europe was struggling to recover from that terrible conflict. Their people had been farmers too, but the climate and soil here in New York were a bit different.

Perry's first memories of *Nona* and Gramps were the warmth of the kitchen, and the smell of home cooking with a European twist. They made their own wine, which Dad said was 'passable', which meant it was okay to drink, and they raised chickens. Chickens were a staple in Italian cuisine, and many famous dishes like *lasagna* were prepared by Nona for Sunday Night Dinner—which is an American custom. The family was the center of life for the Carbones, and their only daughter, Lisa, who was Perry's Mom.

They had particular affection for Perry, their grandson. They spoiled him rotten. They loved Gabrielle too, of course, but it was tradition to pass on the land to the sons. That's just how it was in European culture, especially Mediterranean culture. It was what Perry would remember: *familia*. Home.

"Looka that!" Gramps said, watching the news on TV.

"Hey, Perry, this might interest you. It's about science, geology specifically."

Robert Normal, CFA, was always encouraging Perry to be aware of what was going on in the world, as he put it. A financial analyst, his world was rising prices of commodities, investment counselling, and the economy in general. He either read the newspaper—preferably <u>The New York Times</u>—cover to cover, or watched National News coverage on TV, or both.

"It's Yellowstone Park." Perry was sitting next to Gramps and his father on the sofa.

"It's gonna blow up, say the newsman." Gramps was cleaning his glasses with a tissue, and squinting at the screen. "How they gonna do that?"

"No, Gramps, 'they' are not going to blow it up. It's a supervolcano. It blows up by itself every few thousand years. It's due for a big eruption soon, geologists say."

"Isn't this just talk, Perry? Yellowstone has been a geothermal vent for hundreds of years," queried Perry's father. "Why would that change?"

"They discovered another huge magma chamber under Yellowstone, Dad. The whole park is one big ancient caldera. They've been measuring earthquake activity there lately and it has increased dramatically.

Now the public has found out and they are worried. Some people say that it will wipe out a third of the United States if it has a Magnitude 5 eruption."

Perry knows what that is like. He accidentally time-traveled back to the fateful week of the Santorini eruption that ended the Minoan culture in Greece in two terrible days.

But he wouldn't say that if you asked him. He hasn't told anyone about that yet. Some secrets are better left alone.

"Surely the government is aware of the danger it poses; they will be prepared, no doubt."

"I'm not so sure, Dad. Just this week the federal government and the military spoke out and came up with a plan that sounds ludicrous."

"Go, Bills!"

Gramps had changed to the Sports Channel and was cheering for his favorite team, the Buffalo Bills. Gramps was kind of a football fanatic. He liked soccer and FIFA World Cup, and he liked NFL pro ball as well.

That's why he had a satellite dish mounted outside on the farmhouse wall. Over 300 channels. Lots of sports to watch.

Chapter Two   Giving Thanks

Perry and Henry were in Science class. The teacher had proposed that two teams have an official debate, in the school auditorium, on a current issue in Science. Perry was on one side, and his best friend Henry on the other. It was going to be classic.

"State your thesis clearly, teams. Perry, first."

Mr. Matson was the referee. He made the microphone squeal when he first picked it up. They all do that. The principal. Everyone.

"We declare that Yellowstone Park is a positive danger to the United States, and should be closed to the public until further notice." Perry spoke in a very concise way. Typical Perry.

Then it was Henry's turn. On Henry's team was Max, Robert, Margot, Charmaine, and Rowan. They were strong contenders for any debate, and they were hot to trot.

"We declare that Yellowstone Park is as safe as it has ever been, and to close it would lose the

National Park Service thousands of visitors, and lots of money."

"Yeah, baby!" Henry's team was being vocal. They didn't need cheerleaders at all. Many students in the auditorium cheered and whistled. Mr. Matson raised his hand.

"Opening arguments: Perry's team." Mr. Matson was enjoying this as much as the students; you could see it in his face.

"First of all, learned colleagues, let me point out the geological facts about Yellowstone Caldera, and its current state of unrest," Perry began.

"Yellowstone is a ticking time bomb sitting on one of the most dangerous hotspots in North America. That includes the Alaskan volcanoes, which are in constant eruption."

Perry explained the situation so that the audience, sitting in the auditorium, would be able to understand what was going on, and why Perry believed it was important to know about.

The rules said no Powerpoint or visual aids, just good old argument, well-presented and well-stated. Those were the rules.

Just like when Perry's Dad went to Brackendale, like, a thousand years ago.

Henry's team was very persuasive.

What evidence of this mega-eruption was there?

Swarms of earthquakes happened all the time in the region of the Rocky Mountains and the Grand Teton range.

Old Faithful was still behaving as a geyser should, venting steam in regular intervals, drawing 'oohs' and 'ahhs' from the tourist crowds watching inside the park.

But Perry had saved his sharpest arrow for the end.

"If there is no danger, no risk, as my learned colleague Henry proposes, then why has NASA announced this very week that they have a plan to drill miles into the rock and inject water to cool the magma so it *won't* erupt?"

A murmur ran through the crowd like a wind.

"I'm sure they have a perfectly good reason, I suppose." Henry was faltering.

"Can you guess what would happen if cold water meets 3000 degree molten lava? I don't think that would avoid the trouble; I think it would blow the lid right off Yellowstone Park," Perry exclaimed.

The crowd went nuts. Almost every student jumped to his or her feet, and let his or her emotions out with shouts and catcalls.

Mr. Matson was powerless to stop it. So he just sat down and waited it out.

Perry had timed it perfectly.

Once the crowd quieted down, Perry stood up to the mic, and softly said: "If the government of the United States thinks this primeval fire, burning in the bowels of Wyoming and Montana, is serious enough to be extinguished by any means, ladies and gentlemen, we have a really big problem. America is in trouble. And everyone in this room, in this town, in this state, in this country, will be affected in ways that are unimaginable. Thank you."

And Perry Normal, junior scientist, scholar, and excellent public speaker, sat down.

For one breathless moment, the entire room was silent, taking in the impact of his words. Then all hell broke loose.

Students were climbing over seats, pushing and shoving and laughing, shouting, singing uncontrollably. It was bedlam.

They streamed out the doors into the corridor, or out the emergency exit doors in the wings. The combined energy of nearly three hundred students could have literally raised the roof, had it not been firmly attached to the walls of the school.

The football team lifted Perry on their shoulders, like he was the king of something. Singing the school song, they triumphantly marched out to the field, and the school day was pretty much over.

The Principal spoke briefly to Mr. Matson, but they were grinning, so it must have been okay.

***

Renee Marchmount was new to Brackendale, having transferred from a school in Portland, Oregon early in the term. So, of course, she had no friends, no easy way into the inner circles at school.

People said that she was introverted, a bit weird; they sensed it and were a bit cold to her at first.

But she was smart—really smart. She got 108 out of 108 on the Science midterm at Brackendale and her Math marks reflected her remarkable intelligence. That got the immediate respect of Henry and Perry, the leaders of the nerds who made up the Science Club at Brackendale.

"Renee? We would like to formally invite you to be in the Science Club," said Perry.

"Really? What do you guys do?" Renee expressed interest.

"We discuss important areas of scientific inquiry, and new and exciting discoveries that don't make the front page of the papers," Henry said.

"We subscribe to the idea that Science has answers to everything, " said Perry. "All phenomena can be explained by using scientific inquiry to reveal the hidden mechanism that underlies the Universe," he went on.

"That's Newtonian thinking," Renee said. "That may or may not gibe with Reality, as Einstein suggested."

"Do you know what an Einstein-Rosen Bridge is?" Henry blurted out. "Perry built one in his basement and it....". Perry cut him off quickly.

"It was a project for the Science Fair last year, but was just a model."

"Yeah! A model that won Perry first prize and a trip to New York City!" You could tell by the animated expression that Henry was still up in the clouds about it.

"I see," said Renee, looking at Perry with steady grey eyes.

Perry felt her gaze, but did not look away. There was something *about* this girl; Perry wondered if the gang would feel the same way.

The noise at The Malt Shop was deafening. Everyone was talking and gossiping and wolfing down the amazing food that the restaurant served, so much better than the school cafeteria, and cheaper. Not to mention homemade, with love.

Dave owned the restaurant but his wife and daughter did most of the cooking. Dave was fat because he liked eating. He knew the food was good too.

"Hey, people! This is Renee. She's new and she's cool." Perry's words were like the Supreme Court of the United States speaking. If Perry said it, it was to be considered authoritative and final.

"Hi, Renee!" The whole gang was in: Robert, Charmaine, Margot, Rita, Max, Katya, and of course, Henry.

"Hello," she replied shyly. "This is where you hang out?"

"Man, this is our real home," said Max exultantly, and almost meant it.

"Where are you staying, Renee? Can we come over sometime?" Margot had turned and leaned closer to Renee.

"I am living with my aunt right now. I wasn't getting along with my mom and we made an arrangement."

"Where's your dad?"

"He and my mom split and he went to Seattle to work. He never writes. He never sends money. Not even at Christmas."

"That sucketh," said Robert. Everyone agreed.

"We'll be your family, Renee." Margot was leaning into the booth, eyes bright with emotion. "You won't walk alone." Again, murmurs all around of assent.

"Thank you. I really appreciate it." Renee caught the tear before it slipped from its perch on her left eyelid.

"Fries?" offered Robert, who ate every chance he could get, so he had, like, six meals a day.

***

Thanksgiving was coming. Perry wanted to invite Renee, but had no idea how to do it tactfully.

First of all, he should, by rights, invite her Auntie as well.

He didn't want them to feel like charity cases or something, who couldn't afford a turkey dinner of their own or who didn't have any social network in town.

Perry was not very skilled at social event organizing even though he was President of the Science Club. You had to have experience in these things.

He could ask his Mom, Lisa, since she did this stuff at the School Board from time to time. But he was a bit shy about asking her.

Then his mom will want to know what is special about Renee and he wasn't eager to share his feelings with anyone right now.

The time window to invite her was closing, and Perry was uncharacteristically nervous.

His mind wasn't on the chemistry experiment, which required him to perform paper chromatography on an unknown sample provided by the teacher.

His lab partner was pretty clueless, so Perry felt responsible. He pulled it off, but fumbled with the equipment, and nearly contaminated the sample with apple juice.

"Perry? What cloud is your head in at this precise moment?"

He got English class, after Science class. Miss Busby, the English teacher, was addressing Perry halfway through a lesson on the significance of Setting in poetry, and literature in general.

"Maybe it's not in a cloud," muttered The Gorilla. "Maybe it's up his—".

Miss Busby gave The Gorilla a withering look.

"...sleeve," he finished lamely.

27

"Sorry, Miss Busby. What were you saying?" Perry looked up.

Everyone had noticed Perry was distracted lately. Charmaine said it was Renee. Margot wondered if he was getting the flu, like most students in the late fall. Henry didn't notice, but then, Henry was kind of spaced out much of the time himself.

"Setting is intrinsic to literature, just like excitement is intrinsic to sport."

"Eh?" Robert remarked.

"It gives a mood, provides emotional context for the characters to interact."

"She's talking about The Malt Shop, man," Mike said. "Context for us to interact."

After class, at the Malt Shop, everyone agreed that English class was becoming more and more annoying as the concepts and vocabulary became more incomprehensible.

Charmaine offered her generic rant: *'Why do we have to take English anyway?'* etc., etc.

That gave Perry a brief window in time to ask Renee 'The Question'.

But it was not the invitation to Thanksgiving dinner he had been planning to make.

Not at all.

"I was thinking, Renee. Ah, maybe we could, like, go out, spend time together—just the two of us. I have never had a girlfriend, never thought about it, actually. But I really like you a lot. I mean *really*. "

There! The secret that he was holding in burst out, and nobody heard it because they were all agreeing with Charmaine, or blabbering their own opinions in the happy relaxed way people did at The Malt Shop: their home away from home.

But Renee *had* heard. She studied Perry with her amber eyes that made her look a bit wild, like a lynx or cougar.

Then she smiled—not a grin mind you -- but it told a story on its own.

It made Perry reach across the table and take her hand. A simple gesture, really. But a bold statement on Perry's part.

"Buy me a ring?" she said.

"Okay, sure. What kind of ring?"

"Amethyst. My favorite. Symbol of The Higher Self. Spiritual awakening."

"We can go on Saturday to The Crystal Shoppe. Oh. I forgot. That's Thanksgiving."

Perry went on.

"Ah, I asked my mom if there were, if we could have company for dinner on Saturday. She said okay."

"It's alright. We can go get it maybe next weekend."

"No! I mean, yeah. What I want to say is: will you and your aunt come for Thanksgiving dinner at our place. Please?"

Renee looked far away for a moment.

"I'll have to ask her, but I think it will be fine," she said.

The smile was back, and a little brighter and her hand gripped his a little tighter.

"Thank you very much, Perry."

"We can pick you up," Perry said.

"We have a car. And GPS. What time should we come?"

CHAPTER THREE   MOONLIGHT IN VERMONT

"She's a lovely girl," said Perry's Mom.

"Yes. Yes, she's very nice," said Perry's Dad.

Having his parents' blessing was the icing on the cake.

"Her aunt is a riot," said Gabrielle. "After two glasses of wine, she was even funnier."

"Hush!" said Lisa to Gabby. "Let's not make judgments on people."

The dinner was one of the best ever, thought Perry. Mom could cook a turkey like nobody could and Nona made pasta, instead of potatoes, on the side.

Best of all: Perry got to sit beside Renee and hold her hand under the table. If anyone noticed, they didn't let on.

Christmas was coming and the whole school was arranging holiday decorations or events by homeform.

Miss Busby's 7E class was going to perform a parody of 'The Twelve Days of Christmas' onstage. Several students would play guitar and flute accompaniment; Randy The Gorilla, it turned out, was a closet bass player who wasn't half bad. He turned red when someone put his name forward, but his buddy Mike nailed him down for the concert, and that left Perry and Renee and Margot and Max to come up with silly lyrics that reflected the spirit of both Christmas, and of Brackendale Middle School.

"*On the first day of Christmas, my true love gave to me, a partridge in a pear tree,*" became "*...a sneak peek in a pear tree,*" which Miss Busby nixed as too suggestive, so they hemmed and hawed until after dinner time to get something they could all agree on.

Snow was falling just like in a Robert Frost poem. The forest along County Road 13 was becoming 'lovely, dark and deep' as December came.

That is near where Perry's home was, and further down the valley, was his grandparents' farm, a place of happy summer memories.

Christmas lights could be seen across the valley as the joyous festive season came to Brackendale. Children were too excited to sleep at night. Including Perry. He had a special plan for this Christmas, a surprise that involved Renee, the girl who won his heart.

***

Perry's email set the stage.

To Renee Marchmount <reborn1995@yahoo.com>
                    Dec 17 at 10:41pm

Dear Renee: I want to share an adventure this holiday season. I will need you to be completely available to travel to a faraway land called Vermont from Boxing Day until New Year's Day on an organized tour. I will pay for everything. Just say 'yes' or 'of course, darling!' or something, ASAP. With love, Perry.

She did; but somebody at school snitched. Somebody found out about the romantic holiday. *Somebody must die!* Perry fumed.

Turned out it was the least likely person to keep a secret, as Perry knew from summer camp: Henry!! Perry had confided his plans for a ski vacation in snowy Vermont, with little inkling that the whole of Grade 7 would be given a new topic of gossip.

"Have fun on your little holiday, Perry," Charmaine and Katya and Margot teased.

The Gorilla chimed in: "Don't do anything I wouldn't do!" with an evil grin.

"Text me," said Max and Robert with one voice, like somebody with two heads talking.

"Ok sure," Perry said. "I've never gone skiing and neither has Renee. Should be interesting-- if we don't kill ourselves."

"Don't do *that*," Henry said. "Try to estimate the median winter precipitation in that area, or bring me some National Park flyers or brochures. You know I collect stuff like that."

"Sure thing, Henry."

"Photos!! E-mail photos or post online!" His friends seemed more excited than he was.

"Merry Christmas, everyone!" Perry's face was beaming like the plastic Santa Claus in the school foyer. Then Friday came, and school was on recess for two and a half glorious weeks.

***

Perry bought his Dad socks. He always did. His Dad always liked the socks. Maybe it was an accountant thing—get something simple and practical.

He got his mom and his sister new slippers, on sale at Penny's, but who would care? It was always a special moment when December 25 arrived, and there was stuff in pretty paper under the tree. Didn't matter how old you were; Christmas was special. Unwrapping, and smiles of delight, and Mom's pancakes for breakfast.

Later, Perry packed for the trip. Fleece jacket, ski jacket, wool socks, winter boots. They could rent ski equipment at the hill. Mittens instead of gloves, because mittens kept your fingers warmer. He bought an expensive pair for Renee, size XS, with fake leather padding on the palms and thumbs. For the grip.

"We know you will behave like a gentleman, Perry," said his father. "You and Renee are just friends and for now, that's probably best."

"Remember. If anything happens, call." That was his Mom. She was such a 'mom'.

Gabby slipped him two hundred in twenties, 'just in case'. She pulled him aside so Mom couldn't hear.

"You got protection?"

At first Perry failed to register what was being said.

"You know? Condoms?" Gabby was glaring into his face just like a big sister does.

"Oh, we aren't planning to do...that." Perry was shocked. Did his sister really think they were doing stuff like that? They were only in 7th Grade. He had only kissed her once, and it was fleeting. No french kisses.

To Perry's eternal amazement she thrust a small crinkly package into his jacket pocket and zipped it firmly.

"You can thank me later."

Perry mumbled something incoherent then Dad said the Jeep was warmed up and that they should go meet the bus.

Renee was waiting at the Greyhound station on Center Ave. as they pulled in.

"Here." Perry's dad passed him a further two hundred-- in small bills. "Have fun, son."

Then his Dad did something inexplicable, according to Newton's Laws of Thermodynamics. He hugged Perry, and kissed him on the forehead.

When Perry got out of the Jeep, the cold wind froze that spot into a memory of how great his family was. He would miss them.

The two lovers stowed their gear in the overhead bins and snuggled down into the seats near the back of the coach. In the next three stops the bus filled with happy couples, mostly kids from college or private schools. You could always tell *them* by the expensive clothing like Helly Hansen skiwear or Armani jackets made for the city shopper to show off in. They were all headed to the White Mountains--the American mecca for skiers in the East. Others go to Quebec, to Mont Tremblant, which has longer runs and a later closing time for the bars.

Tours like this are big business in this part of the world. Travel companies all compete for this narrow window at New Year for the same demographic. Perry hoped they could go to Canada next year, if all worked out as planned in Vermont.

The resort was just as nice as the website said—complete with hot tubs and all the amenities. After a six-hour bus ride, they needed to let off steam, sothey found their room and starting jumping on the beds like two little kids. This ended in a pillow fight, which exhausted them both. Renee took a hot shower, and Perry chatted with Henry online.

Dinner was a tour-organized affair, so they got to meet other kids on winter break.

"Hi, I'm Perry, this is Renee."

"Hi, I'm Andy and this is Mario and his sister Maria, from Brooklyn. We have never been in the mountains, or in a nice hotel like this. And no parents! This is totally awesome!"

"Good evening, everyone, I am Holly—your tour guide on this trip. The buffet is open and the food is hot; just a reminder that everyone is hungry so try to limit what you eat for the first hour so everyone gets to eat. There's a bar if you have ID. We leave the hotel at 9:30 a.m. for the White Mountains ski day so don't be late please."

"Man, she sounds like a teacher," said Rob, a tenth grader from Fernville.

"She *was* a teacher, until she lost her job in the cutbacks."

Billy came from Tonawanda High School, and was traveling with a couple of rowdy football players who were hoping to meet girls and do all kinds of things you do when there is minimal control and virtually no adult supervision. Imagine camp—without the counselors!

"I'll bet she was fired for being part of a child-sex ring, or a Satanist," offered Jerry, who was from Rochester.

"Sounds like you're describing yourself, Jerry," Billy said with a smile.

"Yeah, right. It's going on my resume once I finish the training."

The banter died down as the plates filled up with delicious food.

Someone had correctly assumed that teenagers care less about fine cuisine and more about good-old rib-sticking dishes like spaghetti with meat balls, three-topping pizza, cheeseburgers, fries with gravy, deep fried chicken legs, and endless refills on soft drinks with ice.

"Are you worried about tomorrow?" Renee studied Perry's expression.

"A little. I need some lessons. I tried nordic skiing one time and could not keep the skis parallel, and ended up having to flop into a snowbank to stop myself on a short hill."

Renee giggled and her eyes sparkled.

"I never imagined this! You totally caught me by surprise. Was this something you just cooked up, or were you daydreaming in class?" she said.

Now it was Perry's turn to smile.

"I never imagined myself doing something like this when I was younger. But I've had some...experiences, you could say...that have showed me a bigger picture. Maybe it's something my Granddad said: 'Do it while you're young'. Anyhow, my parents were great about it all. So here we are."

Perry clinked his glass of cranberry cocktail against Renee's glass. To his surprise, and delight, she leaned into his collar and quickly kissed his cheek.

***

Holidays were for sleeping in, so it came as no surprise to anyone that the tour would be leaving 30 minutes late. Holly was stamping her boots in the lobby, and kids were boarding the bus, then abruptly coming off to get someone, then climb on again. Finally she did the head count, and the big tour coach rumbled out onto the blacktop.

For two hours the bus would wind its way into the heart of New England's winter wonderland and the snow would fall like curtains around them.

The experienced ones lined up quickly to rent gear and get out on the chairlift. The others milled about trying to figure out the sequence of how to get on the darn thing.

"Ok, people. Collect the stuff you need, line up with your $20, and we'll meet over on the landing below the chairlift in twenty-five minutes. Let's not waste our time here, folks."

Holly would remain at the bottom of the ski hill and orchestrate the whole affair.

Renee's turn came. "Size 5 boots, I guess. I'm five feet five so I need the women's ski and poles." She toddled off and Perry soon followed.

"How do I use the poles, Perry?"

"I guess you use them to help steer. Most of the work is done by your legs, knees, and ankles as you twist the skis and try to hold them together. The whole thing is weird when you think of the physics involved. You need muscles you never knew you had."

Holly was shouting to one kid "Get off, just get OFF."

"He's afraid of heights," one girl said.

The boy half jumped, half fell off the chair before it took him further upslope.

The jocks were laughing at him, and throwing snowballs, until Holly yelled.

"You go first, Perry, I'll follow what you do." Renee whispered.

Perry had never been on a chairlift, but had observed that the timing had to be right, so when the chair wheeled into position, he hopped like a frog onto the plastic seat and grabbed the bar with his free hand.

You had to keep the skis lined up, he realized, so he shouted that to Renee, who was just settling in, two chairs directly behind his.

And suddenly, they were airborne!

The feathers of snow swirled around their faces and stuck on Renee's goggles. She brushed them away and shouted to Perry.

"Oh my gosh, are we really going to do this? How do we get down?" She was breathless with the cold and the thrill of hanging hundreds of feet above the dark forest below.

"We go down on the ski slope, silly! That's the point."

"What if I change my mind?"

"It's okay. Let's see how we feel at the top."

When they got to the 3000-foot level, the chair slowed, and tossed them out like candies in colored wrappers. Some boys with snowboards had already dashed to the slope, leaned way out—and poof! Gone like greased bananas!

"Let's stay together!" Renee was insistent.

The tendency for beginners is to lean back on their skis, so as they started down, most found themselves falling more than moving. But it was fun.

Eventually they skittered to a stop; then, joined the line to get on the lift again.

Perry shared some water with Renee, finding that thirst was a common symptom of strenuous outdoor activity.

"My legs are tired, Perry. Can this be our last run?" Renee was having trouble keeping her skis under control.

"Sure. Let's go down over there near the edge of the Green Run. We won't get in anybody's way. We can take it as slow as we need to. The bus doesn't leave until five. That's an hour and a half. Come on."

The two edged their way out of the main trail, now littered with novice skiers who wiped out at various stages of the run. Most were taking selfies and laughing like idiots.

It was quiet over there, near the trees.

"Let me adjust your helmet and goggles." Perry was also checking her bindings.

Suddenly harsh weather arrived. The wind and sleet were blinding as Perry shot ahead down the curving but gentle slope.

Visibility was less than a couple of yards and Renee would be right behind. He tucked his head under his right armpit to look back-- but everything was white.

No red down jacket, no dark goggles. No Renee!!

Perry made it pretty much down to the bottom before he could turn and have a decent look. Still no

Renee! She had either fallen or wiped out near the top.

"Help!" Perry shouted to a young woman in a ski patrol uniform.

"My girlfriend has not made it down; this is her first time. Can you check on her?"

"She's on the Green trail?"

"Yes, yeah, the one I just came down on."

The patrol girl called in on her walkie-talkie to HQ.

"Yeah, Willy, we got a possible injured on Green Zone 4. Can you get the snowmobile over here fast? OK, thanks."

The Ski-doo responded quickly and they zig-zagged upslope to where Perry thought he had started from. No Renee.

"I see sloppy tracks heading down the Blue," said Karen, the ski patrol officer.

She looked at Perry.

"Is it possible that she got mixed up and followed the Blue trail, thinking that's the route you took?"

"I doubt it. She was right behind me."

Visibility was even worse now. A few hundred feet of elevation means a temperature drop of several degrees and the wind had veered to the north. Perry was shivering, not just from the cold.

The ski patrol team eased its way down the Blue trail, which passed between two lines of trees, making it a more dangerous route, requiring more expert skill.

"There!" The male officer shouted, pointing to a heap beneath a tall spruce.

Perry turned white as wax, and everyone knew this was going to be bad.

Karen radioed. "Call in a chopper, Willy. Vector it on my GPS. And call an ambulance, and the regional medical ER. Make it happen!"

Karen, it turned out, was a senior ranger and patrol officer for this site, and when she spoke, people jumped to action.

"Is...she...?" Perry was choking on his words.

"Check her vitals. Get her bindings loose, Rob, and get her out of those boots."

Renee was unconscious, her face a tangle of blood and hair and snow. Perry was breathing hard as he knelt on the crust of ice beside her limp body.

"I'm sorry, baby, I'm sorry. Please don't die. Renee! Please! I'm here, Renee."

Perry had his gloves off and was rubbing her frigid hands.

Where are your mitts? Where is your ring? He pushed his gloves on over her stiff fingers and knuckles.

The wind flew into a rage as the helicopter dropped into the cleft between the trees. It would not land, so Karen and Willy lashed her into a stretcher and they watched as she was winched up, and the door slid shut, as the helicopter shot straight up and out into the air above the valley.

Darkness was falling when the tour bus arrived back at the resort. Perry was silent as he took the elevator up.

Chapter Four   So Alone

"Do you want us to come get you?" It was Perry's Mom.

"No, Mom. No. I want to be here. This is where we planned to have this time together. I don't want to...change anything. It's paid for, anyway, I don't want to waste Dad's thousand bucks."

"Perry, it's not about the money. We just want you home."

"What am I gonna tell her Auntie Bea? This is going to look like my fault, which it is. What a stupid idea! What was I thinking? She couldn't ski and I made her. I'm such a loser."

"Perry, it was *not* your fault. It was an accident. This is a sport, and like any sport things can go wrong. I will call Aunt Bea. You text us any news, ok? You will be back next week. Is there someone you are friends with there, that you can, you know, talk to?"

"I'm ok, Mom. I'll let you know the minute I find out anything. Thanks, Mom. I love you."

"Oh, Perry, we love you too. Be brave my scientist! It will work out somehow. Ok? Bye darling."

Perry's cell chimed LO BATT, so he plugged it in, and slipped between the cool sheets, alone in the darkness of a winter's night.

***

The medical center was a half hour by taxi from the resort.

Renee was in ICU.

"Are you family?" The nurse was filling out forms.

"Kind of. Not exactly. I'm her boyfriend. I was with her."

"Wait here." She returned with the nursing supervisor.

"Hello," she began. "Please sit down.

Your friend is badly hurt. She is still unconscious. There has been bleeding inside the cranium which has put pressure on the cerebrum; that is to say, the part of the brain that would be involved in waking consciousness."

"How long...will she...get better?" Perry's voice cracked.

"We can't say at this point. We're going to transfer her to a brain trauma center closer to home for you, in Albany."

"Should I wait...?"

"I think there's nothing more that you can do here, Perry. Can you get back home on your own?"

Perry tapped his keypad. "Hello, Mom? I think I need a ride. Will you come?"

Even Gabby came-- to comfort Perry on the long drive back to Brackendale. The shock was still affecting Perry and he refused the snack and drink she brought.

Once home, he went straight to his room and closed the door. Perry was not all right. Night had fallen.

***

The whole school held a raffle to raise money for Renee's rehabilitation.

This shows you what kind of people they are. Nobody knew when she would return to school or normal life, but it didn't matter. She was one of them and every student, teacher and administrator felt a communal empathy that made the long winter warmer in Brackendale, New York.

Perry went to Albany once a week with his mother. She knew this was necessary for both Renee, and for her son. The grim fact was that Renee had not returned to consciousness although her vital signs were strong. And her prognosis was otherwise good. Doctors felt confident that the latest MRI scans told the true story: that she would recover at some point, without significant brain damage.

They expected there would be behavioral changes. She might not be the same girl that she was before the accident reported the psychological team to Perry and his Mom, and Renee's Auntie. Renee would need lots of support to return to 'normal'.

Perry tried to be brave, and quipped: "My name is Normal. If anyone is 'normal' it's me." But he had misgivings.

Would she even recognize him? Would she remember that he loved her, and that they were involved in a middle-school relationship that was their first crush?

Perry began to attend church with Nona and Gramps. Not since he was a little boy did he see church, and Christian belief, as a moral and religious model on which to guide one's life. But Perry was determined.

If God existed, then maybe it was time to become better acquainted with what the Bible said, what Christ said, about God, about Life and Death, and Salvation. It was time to look for some answers.

Perry wanted to know where Renee was right now: asleep, or dreaming? Do people in a coma have any awareness? Can they hear people who talk to them? Perry heard that once, from somebody on TV.

Like everything else there were myths and tales about altered states of consciousness. There was also solid science and medical evidence for Perry to investigate and try to explain what happens when we are not in our regular alpha brainwave state.

Perry would look anywhere, follow up any leads, that might help his friend.

His visits to the trauma recovery facility continued on schedule, becoming part of his routine. He was not able to spend so much time with the gang at The Malt Shop, or with Henry, his good buddy. He kept more to himself. This was changing him, pulling him inward.

The school counselor suggested he see a professional counselor, a therapist. Perry didn't want to be seen as a freak, or crazy in some way. But he couldn't deny he wasn't his same old optimistic self. Maybe he needed a holiday.

***

"Sit down, Perry."

Dr. Ginger Friedman was a psychotherapist, meaning she helped people with the mild emotional problems that were part of everyday life for many Americans.

"So, what brings you here today, Perry?" She seemed friendly enough, as she sat across a small table from Perry with a notepad on her knee.

"People think I have changed for the worse since my friend had her accident."

"What do *you* think, Perry?"

"I don't feel that happy at the moment. I would feel a lot better if the doctors told me Renee was recovering, that she wouldn't remain in a coma."

The word stuck in his throat. It was like a shot fired at close range.

"Why don't you tell me the whole story, from the beginning."

***

Renee was on her back in a darkened room in the Children's Critical Care ward of the hospital in Albany. The CCC. Where nobody ever wanted to go, because you would be either a patient or the loved one of a patient in serious medical distress.

The life support machine made a repetitive wheezing sound, her nose and mouth had plastic tubes taped to them so the air could go in and out; it was a scene that struck terror into Perry's heart.

She was barely alive and some machine was breathing for her because she couldn't do it for herself.

Perry did the same thing every time he visited: he would take her hand in his, and start to talk, softly and insistently.

He told her what he was doing that week, and what had happened at school, and what gossip was floating about that involved their colleagues and friends.

Somehow the time flew by, and then visiting hours were over, and Perry had to say 'goodbye'. This was always the hardest part.

Renee had been knocked unconscious and had remained that way for three weeks now.

He was feeling desperate. The longer someone stays in a coma the less likely they will ever come out of it.

To Perry, it was worse than if she had died. She was a prisoner of her damaged body and brain, kept there by medical technology that was wonderful, and yet...she was not really Renee at this moment.

And if she came back to waking consciousness, would she be as she *was*? The happy girl that loved her art classes, and shared that joy with her friends? The girl that captured Perry Normal's heart? His first love.

And there she lay in that cursed bed.

"Come on, Perry. The nurse says it's time to go."

His mom's voice brought him out of his trance and out of the shadow of Room 407.

"Let me tell you something I heard a long time ago, when I was first married to your father. It was called The Serenity Prayer. It goes like this:

God grant me the Serenity to accept the things I cannot change, Courage to change the things I can, and the Wisdom to know the difference.

"This little prayer has been helpful to me many times, Perry.

Now let it help you realize that things happen in Life, things not of our choosing, and beyond our control. But we must go on living all the same. Try to remember that, dear. Please."

It had been a while since Perry had prayed. Too many daily activities seemed to gobble up the time that might be spent in the silent company of the Lord.

Besides, it was mostly his grandparents who went to church, and Perry tagged along because his parents wanted him to have their good influence. Or something like that. He wasn't totally sure.

He was sure that he believed in God, even though there was no actual proof—scientifically speaking—that God existed (#1), that God cared if we messed up our lives (#2), and that turning to God for help would improve anything down here on Earth, (#3).

Perry could not be sure of anything. But he knew that when he prayed very deeply, a warm light came into his closed eyes and a feeling of calm reassurance came into his heart.

Maybe that was what the Serenity Prayer really was saying. Pray. And trust.

But it didn't change the fact that you were still alone when tragedy strikes, when setbacks come, and you feel depressed and helpless. Could prayer fix *any of that*?

CHAPTER FIVE FACE YOUR ENEMY

Death was not a subject of scientific inquiry. Biology taught that organisms live, reproduce, and die, but focus entirely on the 'living' part, not the 'dying/dead' part.

That topic was seldom discussed, by anyone. Not even Sunday School classes dared raise it. Other than a parable such as the raising of Lazarus, Sunday School was about lessons in moral choice and doing what the scriptures taught.

So Perry went back to see Dr. Friedman, a clinical therapist with a Ph.D in Psychology, and training in counseling. She must have answers.

But so far, all she did was ask a lot of questions. *That's how they are taught to deal with people,* Perry thought.

"Can I ask you a question?" Perry said, seated in Dr. Friedman's office.

"Of course, Perry," she replied.

"Do you believe in Life after Death?"

"You've been thinking about Renee, haven't you?"

"Science and medicine talk about processes that occur while we are alive—but nobody mentions what happens when that all ends. It just ends.

Only, I think Science could do better, could investigate what religion seems to be based on—eternal life, life *after* our life ends."

"It's perfectly normal to have these thoughts, Perry," she said soothingly.

Perry sat up and faced her squarely.

"No, Dr. Friedman, it's not normal *to me.* Don't give me that crap that it's going to be okay. Maybe I am just behaving as ordinary people do but I want real answers! You are a scientist, aren't you?"

Ginger Friedman also sat up and leaned over her desk to look directly at Perry.

"As a matter of fact Perry, Science is beginning to study that possibility—that something exists or possibly exists, after—you know."

Even Dr. Friedman hesitated in the face of Death, the finality, the mystery.

"Please continue," said Perry.

"There have been several clinical reports about so-called NDEs: Near-Death Experiences. There is a special branch of psychology and therapy devoted to cataloguing and studying these cases. Statistically, as many as 3% of Americans have had such an experience. That works out to be several million people, Perry. So medicine and psychology cannot dismiss this as an aberration, as a few crackpots who thought they died and went to Heaven, or whatever."

"They actually *died*?"

"Yes. Cessation of heartbeat, breathing, no brain function. Clinically dead."

"And then?"

"Then they suddenly revived and the life support monitors lit up and beeped to announce their return."

"Return from *where*?"

"Yeah, that's the tricky part. Return from where? We don't know. Of course there are neurologists who argue this was nothing more than a brain-based experience that was caused by hypoxia—a lack of oxygen to the brain after breathing stops."

"And these patients were okay?" Perry said.

"If by 'okay' you mean healthy and functional human beings—yes. They revived and recovered, all under a medical team's care and treatment of course."

"How did you hear about all this, Doctor Friedman?"

"I got interested in it after my former husband, a pediatrician, had a case of a young child who died while in the hospital after a severe brain inflammation. The child was gone for what seemed like hours, but was really only a matter of minutes.

When she awakened, she told the doctors some shocking things that she could not have known, not while she was...dead."

"Like what?"

"She told them about a conversation they had in the Operating Room on the 7th floor of the hospital, trying to decide what to do for her now that her heart had stopped and brainwaves had flat-lined on the EEG machine.

She also told them about a running shoe that was lying on a ledge outside the 8th floor kitchen window.

When they sent an orderly to check, they found the shoe—just as she described it—the style, the brand...everything! It was just impossible for her to know these things."

"What did your husband say to her?"

"Well, he asked her how she knew, and she said she left her body and rose up to the ceiling where she could see them and hear them, but of course, they could not see her."

"So, she was a spirit? Or a ghost?"

"Well, we might say she was in her spirit body. This is difficult to put into medical terms."

"That's just my point Dr. Friedman. If something is occurring outside the realm of scientific or medical knowledge we would not have any way of describing it, would we?"

"I think I'm beginning to get where you are coming from, Perry."

"What about the sneaker?"

"She told Harold, my husband—ex-husband—that she floated out the ceiling and window and could see the street eight stories below—the traffic, the pedestrians, and—the shoe! Lying on the windowsill, eighty feet above the street!"

"This is totally freaky," Perry said.

"Well, you can find out more about these cases from IANDS, an organization that gathers data and studies NDEs. Maybe they can answer questions that I honestly have no idea how to answer."

Perry thanked her, and pulled on his jacket. There was research to be done!

***

"There's even a branch of philosophy called Thanatology, Henry," Perry said to his friend.

"And what about this Near-Death Experience story you told me?"

"That's what I want to find out. Are there more stories of people who died and came back?"

"Kind of weird, if you ask me," Henry said.

The boys were in a booth at The Malt Shop. Hot food was coming, and Henry unzipped his jacket and slid out of it.

"Well this is a can of worms, Perry. If we have to scientifically admit the possibility of life-after-death then we must find proof. And then we may have to admit that spirits are real and the Soul is real, and ghosts and goblins and demons and all the rest are real!"

Henry was getting agitated, but in a good way.

"Well. Let's take it one step at a time, Henry, my boy." Perry was glad he had his best friend to share his thoughts and feelings with. Way better than a shrink, he decided.

"My parents are open to things but I never thought to ask them about this," Henry said.

"I know what you mean, Henry, although my Mom shared a prayer with me one time after visiting Renee in the hospital, so she kind of knows."

"What about that shrink? Is she helping you?"

"Dr. Friedman and I have an understanding, you might say, after our last conversation. She knows what I am thinking, at least. And she had good advice."

"Yeah, take this little pill and you'll feel fine tomorrow."

"No, Henry, she is not like that. She didn't even mention medication. She says she prefers 'talk-therapy'. She says she gets better results."

"Whatever that means," Henry said.

Just then the doors blew open and the gang flew in, bringing cold air and warm smiles.

"Where were you, Perry, in last period?" Rita was demanding.

"Henry and I took the afternoon off," said Perry nonchalantly.

"You *skipped*? You?? Perry Normal, skipped class?"

"I just couldn't face Busby and the whole novel analysis business. I feel worn out."

"Better get a doctor's note for the office!"

"Actually, I got one. I was at the psychologist after lunch, before I met Henry."

Rita, Katya, and Charmaine all squeezed into the opposite bench of the booth somehow, and quickly ordered food and drinks.

Henry and Perry had eaten, but when the fries came, Henry asked the girls to share.

"What is it with the fries here," said Charmaine, "that drives people mad?"

Just then Mike came in, bringing the cold March wind with him.

"Hey Perry! Who's that guy you loaned your bike to?"

"I didn't lend my bike to anybody!"

"That's what I thought. Well some guy must have stole it from wherever you left it and he was riding it on the sidewalk a few blocks back."

"Someone stole my bike? It was just outside?" Perry stood up.

"Well, it's back outside again. I knew this guy must've boosted your bike so I pulled him off, slapped him around a bit, then rode it here. You're welcome!"

"Why do I keep losing things?" Perry said. "Thanks a lot, Mike."

He paid for a burger with the works, as a further thank-you to big Mike.

He and Perry had a close relationship that went back awhile, to when Mike had an unusual experience that only Perry could understand because of what Perry knew about strange things.

Still, Brackendale was full of surprises.

***

As they always did, Perry and Henry sat across from each other at the library, spreading out books and magazines all over the table, scribbled notes and pencils tossed among them. This was their idea of a good time: research on a topic that intrigued them.

' Death' was just another subject of inquiry for the two boys. They had researched the moons of Saturn and Jupiter and Mars, they had investigated the archaeological arguments for lost Atlantis. They had become constant companions over the long days of middle school.

"Ok, here's what I am thinking, Perry. I am going to put together a bibliography of sources for information and discussion of Death, Dying, Terminal Illness, and so on. That will help us focus our study, and help us figure out what is known, and what remains to be discovered."

"Great, Henry, thanks a lot!"

Perry had pulled a book out of the Health & Medicine section of the downtown library, the main one in Brackendale. They had more books than the school library did, and Perry wanted to find books-- before they dove into the endless sea of the World Wide Web.

Books were published, edited, accurate. Sometimes the Internet had random garbage that was merely opinion or sensationalism. As always, Perry preferred *facts.*

The title was <u>On Death and Dying</u> and the liner notes said Elisabeth Kubler-Ross was a world authority on the subject, with years of clinical contact with terminal patients. She pioneered treatment programs in the U.S. to help those who were dying; before that, no one really had much to offer. Perhaps people just wrote them off because they were dying. Dr. Kubler-Ross changed health care with her compassionate approach to facing the unspoken enemy of all living things.

"It says there are stages of dealing with dying, and the inevitable end of life," Perry said. "Look at this, Henry."

The boys sat side by side now, poring over the yellowing pages of an old edition, as the afternoon light faded.

"Want to photocopy it?" Henry said.

"Take a picture with your i-Phone you got for Christmas, Henry. Then download and email me. The five stages she discusses here.

'Anger, Denial, Bargaining, Depression, Acceptance.' Those are the stages people go through when confronted with death," Perry said.

"What does that mean?" said Henry.

"It describes our emotional response to the fear and shock of the reality in front of us. I kinda know what this is like because I felt like I went through something similar, over Renee. I didn't, I don't know how to handle it, Henry.

But anyway, this doctor seems to be saying there is a process you go through. It's like she's saying it's perfectly alright to have those feelings and they come in a particular order so you don't feel out of control or like you've lost your mind." Perry looked down at his hands.

"So it's not like prayers or reading the Bible or whatever. It's more, how shall I say? Scientific." Henry said.

"Yeah, I guess you could say that," Perry said. It is a psychological and physiological reaction that doctors like her have observed, and accepted as rational and normal."

"Well, what about NDEs? Who talks about that?"

"That's what you are going to find out and document in your Bibliography, Henry."

CHAPTER SIX   A GHOST STORY

"Hey, Perry. Have you heard the story of the ghost girl on County Road 13?"

They were sitting in The Malt Shop. It was Thursday after school. Charmaine was speaking.

"No. Tell me." Perry was sipping a hot chocolate, and doodling on the paper place mat that read: 'The Malt Shop: Proudly serving Brackendale since 1958', and had a line drawing of the outside of the restaurant as it looked then, and pretty much as it looked now, including the big neon sign that still lit up at night.

"She went to school here about twenty-five years ago. Miss Floon told us the story."

"Miss Floon? The librarian? I didn't know she talked to anybody, except to chase them out of the library after five o'clock on weekdays," Perry said.

Henry came in and joined in.

"What are we talking about, people?" He ordered a meal.

"Ghosts, Henry," said Perry.

"Cool. I've been reading about dead people—or nearly dead people—for a week now. I guess people who *stay* dead become ghosts, or spirits. Right?"

"Stop interrupting me, Henry," said Charmaine.

"One dark night in the fall, this girl Ricki Lee Coulter went out to a party but had to hitch-hike to get there. It was way out in the country somewhere."

"Her parents let her go?" said Henry.

"Shush," said Charmaine and Katya, who just slid into the booth beside her friend.

"She never made it home, and no one even knows if she made it to the party, because the party was not the kind of party nice girls go to, if you know what I mean."

"Sex and drugs?" Now it was Katya cutting in.

"I guess," said Charmaine. "She was, like, thirteen. I don't know what girls did back in the day, but I can guess what boys did," she said with a mischievous smile.

Robert and Max arrived; they sat down in the booth across the aisle, and were laughing about something.

"Quiet!" said Henry. "Charmaine's telling us a ghost story."

"Really? I like ghost stories, but I don't really believe in ghosts," said Robert.

"I believe in food," said Max, ordering a hot turkey open-faced sandwich with pickles and coleslaw. "Robert?"

"I'll have the same," he said to the waitress, who was sixteen and in Eleventh Grade, and seemed to be a focus of attraction for the boys who come here. Maybe it was something in the water.

"How did she die?" Henry asked.

"Well, that's the thing. She never returned home-- and her body has never been found. Police and the County Sheriff's office had searchers out the next afternoon. The weather suddenly turned bad and they called the search off for three days.

When they resumed the search, the creek was full and the woods were soaking. They even took dogs that tracked a scent for a little distance but stopped at the old bridge and wouldn't go any further."

"Ooooh, this is scary stuff," said Max. "Where did you hear all this?"

Charmaine explained that she stayed after school one day and Miss Floon was commenting on the lightning storm that was brewing outside and then she sat down and told her the story of Ricki Lee.

"That old bat must know lots of scary things," said Max with a mouthful of slaw.

"Was this reported in the papers?" Perry asked.

"I never checked," said Charmaine.

"Why are you telling us this now?" asked Henry.

"My older brother. He hangs out with some guys who take their dirt bikes down the east road to a place with a track that off-roaders sometimes use. He says one evening when the sun had just set they were coming back toward the bridge and saw something."

"Something?" said Robert.

"Yeah. A ghost. They even said it was a 'ghost'. My brother Jerry is not a pussy; he's six foot and strong as a linebacker. But he was white as a sheet, telling me this."

"White as a ghost," said Max jokingly. Then everyone laughed as he choked when some food got stuck in his throat and he coughed like crazy for a moment.

"See?" said Katya. "My Ukrainian grandparents say if you choke when someone is speaking that means it is true—what they're saying is true. It's an old folklore thing."

"What did the ghost do?" said Perry.

"It just appeared—and disappeared-- near the crest of the rise when you come up the county road to the bridge. She was wearing an outfit that looked too fancy for it to be a regular girl walking around out there. She looked out of place, somehow."

Charmaine pulled her sweater closer around her and snuggled closer with Katya. The boys shrugged and finished their sandwiches.

"OK," Henry said. "Perry and I are going to find out if there is an old news clipping or something since we are in the library tonight anyway. We'll let you know what we find out."

"Look, Perry." Henry was twiddling the knob on the microfiche reader. Old newspaper content was transferred to plastic film called microfilm, or microfiche, until computers could scan and index articles, Miss Floon had told their class. This one was dated October 1992 from the *Brackendale Courier,* and read:

Local girl vanishes; police investigating disappearance but come up empty.

They read on. They gave details of the girl and a description of the search but not much more. It did say, however, that she was last seen near the bridge and was wearing a nice dress and shoes, and had a pearl necklace around her neck. Belonged to her dead grandmother, apparently.

"What if we go out there, Perry?" Henry said. "You know that road pretty well, right? Your grandparents' farm is a few miles down that road, isn't it?"

"As a matter of fact, yes, Henry. I even know the bridge but it is a few miles further east than my Gramps' farm. We could spend the night with them maybe, like, on a weekend. I'll ask. Let's see if any other news items relate to this. I'm getting hooked by this story."

***

What happened in the end would not be quite as they had planned.

The whole gang decided they would go with them. That was seven people—eight if Margot could get out of the house with some excuse or other.

Perry wanted to bike the twelve miles to the bridge; Henry wanted to get his Dad to drive them. Robert wanted to take a taxi and offered to pay for it.

"How do we get back, Robert?" said Charmaine.

"We call another taxi, silly!"

"Nice that you're rich!" snorted Charmaine.

"What's the point of having rich parents if you don't spend the allowance they give you?" said Robert. Robert always had plenty of cash in his wallet.

In the end, Robert ordered a van taxi, and convinced him to remain at the location where he would drop them off. Robert said he would pay him twice the fare on the meter.

So it was all set. This Saturday would be dry and relatively warm for this time of the year.

Henry had his GoPro; Rita had her phone, as did Katya.

The moon rose over the trees like a slice of yellow cheese, adding to the mood.

"Are you sure you want to do this?" Katya said nervously. "Maybe this is a bad idea."

But she was overruled by the others, and Max was goofing around with Robert. When the cab arrived, they all piled into the seven-seater van.

It was quite a long way to the bridge, and the moon was quite a bit higher in the sky, and much brighter and whiter than before.

"Stop here," said Perry, at length. "This is the bridge coming up ahead."

The bridge, curiously, was not named; there was no sign, just old moss-covered stone parapets that ran up to the cement abutments, and then the steel and concrete decking that shone in the pale moonlight.

The bridge was about seventy feet across, and the creek could be heard gurgling below in the darkness. It was a short drop of about twelve feet from the bridge to the water.

Max and Robert were hawking and spitting over the rail, seeing who could spit further.

The taxi had pulled off on the shoulder, turned off his motor. The glow of a cigarette could be seen through the windshield.

"What now, Perry?" asked Charmaine.

"Well, let's cross and see what's on the other side. I guess."

Henry had his sport camera turned on, and attached to his head with a headband or strap that allowed him to move freely while filming.

"It's got an infrared setting," he explained. "It sees more than the human eye, especially in the dark."

Just as he said the word 'dark' an owl hooted, and everyone jumped. Owls see in the dark rather well, Perry reminded them.

"Did you hear that?" said Rita. Something else was out there.

"I can't hear anything if Max and Robert don't quieten down," said Charmaine.

The sound of the brook seemed distant and the frogs had stopped their incessant croaking.

"Oh...my...gawd!" said Rita. "Look!!"

At the rise in the road just past the far end of the bridge there was a girl about their age. She was a shadowy figure, and if it weren't for the pearls, and the moonlight, they would have maybe missed her altogether.

"Do you *see* that?" hissed Charmaine in Perry's ear.

"I see something. Could be a girl walking." Perry was rubbing his arms but the goosebumps remained, raised, and cold to the touch.

Even Max had shut up and was standing stock-still in horror.

The figure glided to a point near the far end but would not step onto the bridge deck itself.

It was hard to make out her face.

Then Rita's and Katya's phones flashed at the same time. What they saw was something they would recount and talk about for years to come.

The face of the apparition was sunken, with deep eyes like holes, and shadows where the cheekbones should be.

A white finger was raised from a slender arm -- as if in warning. Or something else.

Her clothing seemed to cling to her phantom form and the unearthly glint of the pearl necklace just made the moment utterly macabre.

Katya screamed -- which woke them all out of their trance -- and they bee-lined it to the van. They pounded frantically on the window; the driver was sound asleep.

They could not stop the shaking and chattering of their teeth all the way back into town.

"Do you believe *now*, Robert," said Charmaine. Her expression was one of horror. Robert said that maybe it was a prank, some one wanting them to believe this bridge was haunted.

"I've got video," said Henry. "The camera never lies."

But right now nobody wanted to see Henry's video. They wanted their homes and beds, and Moms and Dads sitting up waiting.

"See you tomorrow," they said, one by one, as the taxi dropped them on the street outside their houses.

Perry and Henry got out at the corner and bade Robert and Max farewell.

They wanted a few moments to talk and decompress. This was not what anyone expected.

"I don't know what we saw, Henry, but it sure looked real to me!"

"I want to see what the video shows. It should show what we saw and with enhanced imagery. I may have the first scientific proof that ghosts are real, Perry! What do you think?"

"I think ghosts are real; I just don't know if I can believe my own eyes.

I don't know if that was the ghost of a girl who died years ago at that spot or not.

My instinct says it is something supernatural; my mind says...what it always says: wait and see."

Henry turned into his driveway. "Remember the men in black that called on us last Hallowe'en? That was beyond belief. I wish I had photographed those guys."

"Goodnight, Henry," Perry said. "Lock your doors, huh."

"For sure. See you at school."

Perry walked the rest of the way, about a hundred yards, alone. The moon was sinking in the west and the night air was damp and formed an eerie mist on the lawns and woods of Brackendale, New York.

ACT II   WHEN IT RAINS IT POURS

CHAPTER SEVEN   WITHOUT WARNING

"Don't bother the sheep, Perry," Gramps always said.

Gramps said that because Perry had recently learned that sheep are fun to ride. Dig your fingers into their woolly fleece and leap on them like a winter sled. They would panic and take off at a rapid run, carrying whatever was clinging to their back.

It didn't seem to hurt the sheep, and it was loads of fun, Perry thought.

Nona was an amazing cook, and cooked stuff his Mom didn't or didn't know how to-- stuff like lasagna with mozzarella and ricotta, or beef short-rib stew with gnocci, seasoned with fresh basil.

Nona made sure everybody got their fill, so Perry could eat his face off and have seconds at lunch and at supper. "Supper' is what Nona and Gramps called it. Not dinner. It stayed in Perry's mind, so 'supper' had a special meaning for him for the rest of his life.

Perry was looking forward to the end of school in June so he could spend a few weeks on the farm. There were chores to do like burning dead branches and stalks from last season's corn, checking fencelines, splitting firewood.

Fires were fun to build and watch. Every kid knows why campfires are an essential part of camping.

There was hay to stack, bind, and get into the hayloft of the barn so the horses had feed. There were sheep to feed and water and salt licks to place near the stable for them.

Lots to do here, Perry realized. Such a nice change from classrooms and books and the indoor confinement of Brackendale Middle School.

So the news hit like an asteroid impact, shocking, devastating, and final.

Mom and Dad were seated stiffly on the living room couch. They never sat there that way, and Perry and Gabby knew something was terribly wrong.

"We have something to tell you. We know it will be very upsetting. But your father and I think we should be direct and honest about it."

Mom had red eyes and no makeup, and kept wiping her cheeks with a tissue.

"Your grandparents were in an accident on the highway last night, after dark. A farm truck pulled out in from of them, and they couldn't stop."

Perry knew what came next. It was as if time had stopped. He knew Mom couldn't bear to say the awful words, but they came anyways.

"They were both killed. They died instantly the police said. It wasn't their fault. It was just a tragic accident; it could have happened to anyone."

Gabrielle shook with sobs and ran to her mother's arms.

Perry couldn't take all this in. It wasn't real. It couldn't be.

"We will make funeral arrangements for next week." Dad spoke now. "We have to be brave, and carry on doing the things that Nona and Gramps would want us to do."

The pressure of the wave in his body was building.

"NO!" Perry shouted the word. That one word was all he could get out of his throat. He was choking, drowning.

"I have to get out of here!" Perry charged for the door.

He wanted to be alone and not see and not talk -- to anyone.

He found his bike and pedaled furiously toward the bridge. His family lived in an upscale neighborhood near the edge of the town, near a county road that led to farms and forests, away from the busy town. Perry knew this road well. It was the same road that would take him to Nona and Gramps' farm -- if you could pedal eight miles one way.

***

It was nearly dark when Perry reached the farm. He put his bike by the back door, which could not be seen from the road. The key was under the mat, like always. Perry let himself in. That familiar smell was in the kitchen.

So that is where he sat down to think.

"I'll quit school, become a farmer, take over the farm, that's what I'll do."

Perry's mind was going in all directions at once.

"Who'll take care of the sheep, and the horse? What about the apple trees? The cherries would be ready by July. The corn in August."

Perry spoke aloud to the four walls.

"I don't know anything about farming. I'm in seventh grade. I know about computers and books and I just learned about Copernicus and Newton. They weren't farmers either."

The dam was starting to break in his eyes and chest.

No one could hear him; he was safe here and he let the tears and shouting just pour out till there wasn't any left.

He was spent.

Then he remembered leaving his home.

He picked up the heavy black receiver on the phone and dialed his home.

"It's me."

"Where *are* you?" It was Mom.

"At the farm. I'm worried about the animals. They must be hungry and restless. Just let me stay here tonight, Mom. I'll take care of them. I have to take care of them."

"OK, but you are to call me if anything happens, understood? I'll call the school in the morning and say you're sick. I will come out after work around 5:30 to pick you up."

Being a boy, and being eleven, meant parents would sometimes give you permission to do things you couldn't do before. It made Perry proud to be responsible for the farm all by himself, even if it was just for one night. It would be a long night.

"Thanks, Mom. I'm OK. I'll call if I need to."

***

Nothing prepared him for this.

There was no school psychologist or counselors to cushion the blow. There was no shared grief and pain, no one who understood. At least no one Perry's age.

First Renee slams into a tree on their romantic holiday together and ends up in a hospital ward plugged into apparatus that keeps her temporarily alive. For what?

Now his grandparents, who worked hard to support their family and be good decent Americans who immigrated from war-torn Italy. Why did this happen *to them*?

Perry Normal was not the kind of person to run from tough questions. He knew that Science had answers for almost anything.

But Science did not say much about the Good and the Bad, what's Right, and what's Wrong. Humans had to deal with those moral dilemmas.

Religion claimed to have answers to the question of what is the right thing to do. But people still had to make their choices, and suffer the agony of losing people they really loved and needed.

Perry was angry. He admitted it. Not angry at anyone in particular, just supremely pissed off.

And he did not have a plan.

Perry always had a plan but, for once, he was out of ideas, and no plan to get himself out of it, away from the uncertainty that there were things we cannot control or prevent in Life.

Perry felt naked. Like a newborn baby. Now he knew why babies cry when they are born.

***

Perry's parents decided to sell the farm. It was not an easy decision.

"Why? Can't we just keep it and use it as a place to go on weekends?" Perry and Gabby were both on the same side on this.

Perry's Dad was speaking softly.

"A farm is a lot of work. I can't do it, your mother can't do it. It wouldn't be fair to the memory of Nona and Gramps to let it run down. We are not rich enough to afford to hire farmhands and renting brings up other problems."

Perry and Gabrielle realized their parents were right.

Nothing could bring Nona and Gramps back, and all Perry and his family had left were the precious memories of days on the farm, with two of the most wonderful people they would ever know in their whole lives.

"We are going to the farm this weekend to gather the last of the important things left behind.

On Sunday some local men will come to inspect, and hopefully buy, the farm equipment and the livestock. Then the real estate agent will come to look things over and make some suggestions about listing the property," Dad said.

"Let me make some brunch on Saturday morning before we go over," said Mom.

The thought of food made Perry, at least, feel slightly hopeful.

Gabrielle went upstairs to text with her friends but Perry went to her room and quietly knocked

"Gab? Can I speak with you for a couple of minutes?"

"Sure, Perry, come on in. Don't step on my stuff—I haven't had time to organize things since…it happened."

"I know this is not the time to bring this up, but you are the only person I can talk to, Gabby. It's about Renee."

Gabby pulled her chair sideways and wrapped a shawl around her bare shoulders.

"Yeah, that is pretty tough for you to deal with, huh Perry. And now this. You've got more on your plate than I do."

"The thing is, what if Renee...doesn't make it? I know it sounds perverse but as long as she is alive— even if it's in a hospital on life support I have hope. You know what I'm saying?"

"Yeah. The doctors say she might come out of it, right? That's worth hoping for Perry. We have to be optimistic. When do you go again? To see her?"

"Friday afternoon. Mom will take me."

"Can I come?"

"You want to?"

"Yeah, I want to. I want to be with you and Mom, and I want to see her. I just think I should be there one time with you guys."

"Okay. That would be good. I can ask Mom if Renee's Aunt Bea wants to go with us. I don't want her to feel like she's all alone in all this."

"Right." She suddenly hugged her brother and looked in his eyes.

"We're going to get through this, Perry. No matter what happens. Okay?"

Two beads of moisture formed in her eyes.

"Thanks, Sis." Perry stood and showed himself out of her room.

***

"Perry? I want to talk to you after school -- at The Malt Shop." Charmaine was pulling on Perry's sweater.

"What's up, Charmaine," Perry said as they were seated in the familiar booth at the local cafe. The seats had been re-upholstered ten years ago but the owners insisted it be like the original leather, comfy and cozy. Rita slid in beside Charmaine.

"I've got someone you might like to see, Perry. She is a Tarot card reader. She is really good!"

"Tarot? Those fortune-telling cards the Gypsies used to use?"

"Yes. Lot's of people use them now, Perry. They're not weird or anything anymore. You can even get apps for them on Android or iPhone.

This person is amazing. My aunt told me she knew everything about her early life and gave her important advice that turned out to be totally accurate!"

"Why would that be relevant to *me*? Perry replied.

"You want answers, right? To what's going to happen with Renee? Or with your life this coming new year? "

"You're telling me that a pseudoscientific folk method of telling the future is something I should even consider believing?"

"Perry! I know you are Mr. Science and that everything has to have a scientific basis or experimental validity, but sometimes you gotta let go and just trust the Universe will give you something you really need!"

Charmaine was getting emotional. She grabbed Perry by both hands and looked at him.

"Trust *me*, Mr. Perry Normal. I am your friend. Okay?"

Perry thought for a moment, then nodded.

"Okay, then. Wednesday, after school. We meet here. I will bring Rosa with me. You can discuss a price with her. Oh, and bring a tape recorder. You will want to listen to what she has to say later on, when you have some private time. We good?"

"Thanks, Charmaine. I'll be here."

Perry got his bike and pedaled slowly home, his mind awhirl with thoughts of what to say, or what would the fortune teller Rosa say, and what he should do with the information.

Henry. Text me! It's important!

Henry was always very good about answering his best friend's text.

Hey? What's up?

Perry preferred to talk, since texting sometimes seemed so darn slow. Henry's cell chimed its ringtone, a guitar riff from the Sixties' band The Ventures.

"Hey, Perry," said Henry, through a mouthful of something, as usual.

"Can I ask you a favor? Will you come with me on Wednesday to the Tarot card reading at The Malt Shop? Bring your little tape recorder thingy."

"Sure. What time?"

***

Rosa turned out to be a lot younger than the old wizened crone he had imagined. She was a bank manager, in fact. With an MBA. She was friendly and greeted Perry warmly.

"Hold the cards in your hands, both hands, briefly; then 'cut' them three times and place them on the table."

Perry did as he was told.

Rosa methodically placed ten cards, in a pattern called the Celtic Cross, on the white cloth she had placed on the table in the booth.

Charmaine had asked Dave, the owner, for a booth in the rear, where they could be undisturbed. Rosa had asked for a bottle of mineral water.

"The cards respond to your inner thoughts, Perry.

Whatever forces control them, they will point directly at certain events, or actions, that have an effect on your life at this time. I do not control them in any way, as you can see. I just shuffle and deal them off the top."

"Will you tell me what they mean?"

"Of course, I will give my interpretation to the reading. Each position represents an aspect of the Question that you have in your mind today."

So she began.

"First card—the Significator. That means *you*, at this moment in time. King of Swords. This card means you are powerful mentally and use Reason and Judgment to deal with the problems in your life."

Henry murmured, "Yup! That's Perry."

"Sshhh," said Charmaine.

"Second card—the Obstacle, the issue which crosses or blocks your path forward. Four of Swords. Repose. Someone is sleeping, perhaps resting after a trauma."

Perry blinked. Of course this meant Renee. In a coma after the accident.

The third card, at the bottom of the spread, was The Fool. Rosa said this reflected Perry's attitude about Life in general—that he was open to all possibilities, and the card had a picture of a carefree young man about to step off a cliff into the Unknown.

Charmaine sneaked a grin at Rosa, and winked at Henry. So far, so good.

The fourth card was The Lovers. This showed the Recent Past, and the energy that was still present; Perry had to admit that this was on his mind most days.

"It's good that you recognize for yourself, Perry, what the cards are offering in terms of insights into your life." Then Rosa went on.

The fifth card is what is hanging over you, Rosa continued. It was a scary card with a dead guy lying there with ten swords sticking straight out of his back! The card was upside down, unlike the others.

"What is that?" Perry sounded a bit shocked.

"You had a deep loss that brought a permanent and profound change in your life. Does this make sense to you?"

"I lost my grandparents very recently, in a tragic accident."

"Yes. That is what the cards say. But it also means that you will move on with your life, after you process the grief. That is why it is 'reversed'—upside down."

The sixth card was to the right of the Significator. It indicated what will happen in the near future. This card was The Chariot, the seventh card in the Major Arcana—the really heavy-duty cards in the 78 cards of the Tarot deck.

Rosa said this card meant 'Victory through adversity', meaning someone will go through a hard time but will emerge triumphant through the power of their own Will to live.

Perry jumped up and almost spilled his drink on the spread of cards.

"No! Really? Do you realize what this means?!" The veins in his neck were distended and his face was flushed with sweat. "It's about Renee! It *has* to be!"

Charmaine and Henry were all trying to get Perry to sit down again.

Finally he did. Henry patted him on the back saying it would be alright. Charmaine stroked his hand. She had a magical touch, and soon Perry was calm enough to proceed with the reading.

The slanting sun threw bright rays through the blinds onto the tables and floor. Charmaine took it as a good sign.

There were four cards left to read. The first three blurred before his eyes as his gaze was fastened on the final card, The Outcome of the matter in question.

The card was Death.

A skeleton in black armor rides a white horse carrying some kind of banner.

Perry was aghast.

Charmaine covered her mouth, and Henry studied his hands under the table.

"Then she will die?" Perry blurted out.

"Not at all," said Rosa, unperturbed.

"The Death Card does not mean someone dies; it actually means 'transformation' or 'rebirth' or 'renewal'. It means the end of an old life and the beginning of a new one."

Rosa went on.

"Now I don't know if this refers to your friend—Renee, is it? Funny. Her name means 'rebirth', in French. Did you know that?"

"Not really. But keep saying what you're saying. She won't die?"

"Something life-changing will happen—to her, or to someone you know. But dying is not in the cards, so to speak." Rosa smiled.

"Besides, this may not refer to Renee at all. It might refer to you. Or a situation that must come to an end now, because it is time. The energy that sustained the situation has dissipated. So it really does mean a new day, a fresh start."

Perry look relieved, and his friends sighed as the tension of a few moments ago released into smiles and giggles.

Rosa carefully packed her materials, and asked if there were more questions, but Perry honestly had none to ask.

After she had gone, Charmaine took Perry's hand again.

"You are not alone, Perry. You were never alone. We are your friends for always and you will have us to turn to in good times and bad."

She hugged him hard; everyone agreed that the Brackendale 'gang' was the best part of being at school.

When Perry got home he lay down and had a nap, which he almost never did, but he needed to re-group. He had been through a lot lately, he realized. *Just rest a bit*, he thought.

He dreamed again of the Tarot cards, floating in the air before him, then some beautiful music; then he woke up after dark in his room.

Someone tapped on his door and opened it slightly. It was Gabby.

"Hey, sleepyhead! Are you coming down to dinner? It's on the table."

Perry got up and went to splash water on his face and wash his hands.

At dinner everyone was chatting, which was just the right mood for Perry.

He brightened up and soon was eating and laughing with his family, the people that meant more to him than anyone in the world.

***

It was Visiting Day—the day Perry went to see Renee, with his Mom. It was always a tense day, a day with heavy clouds in his heart. Gabby decided to stay home, and Renee's Aunt had a bad cold, and chose not to come either.

He thought about the Tarot reading. There was hope there. There had to be hope because the alternative was unbearable.

He remembered looking closely at the Death Card and had seen the distant horizon lifting in the dawn of something new and exciting. Even on that awful card, there was hope.

Nevertheless, it was a bit of a shock when his Mom met him with the car to begin the journey to

Albany, but did not pull away from the curb right away. She had a smile.

"Perry. We have some good news. Renee has come out of the coma and is awake. She can talk to us! Isn't that great?"

Perry couldn't hold back the tears, and collapsed onto his mother's shoulder.

"We are going to have a special day today, aren't we? Let's get her some flowers," said Lisa. Perry nodded but still was unable to speak at this moment.

When they entered reception, the nurse knew right away that they had received a call from the hospital.

"Congratulations!" she said, and Lisa said, "Thank you so much," as they trod the familiar route to the elevator, then the fourth floor nursing station, then the darkened room down a short hall.

Only now, it wasn't dark. The overhead lights were bright, her bedside table lamp was lit, and the nurse was waiting.

"She woke up in the night," she spoke quietly, "and called for something to drink." The doctor saw her this morning and ordered some tests, including an EEG, which was normal. We think she is going to be okay."

Perry slipped out from behind his mother and moved to the bedside and went down on his knees.

"Renee! Renee! I've missed you. I missed you so much!" Her held her cool hand in the warmth of his.

"Hello, Perry. I was sleeping, wasn't I?"

"Yes, my darling, you were sleeping so long. I was afraid you wouldn't wake up."

"Well, here I am. Why do you call me 'darling'?" She looked puzzled but was smiling.

"It's...how I feel...I am so glad to see you." Perry wasn't sure he could say that he loved her or that he was full of guilt about what happened. This wasn't a time for reflection.

"Oh, Renee! We are so happy to see you back with us," said Perry's Mom, leaning over and giving Renee a quick hug and peck on the cheek.

"Thank you, Mrs. Normal. Where is my Auntie?"

"We will bring her on Saturday. Here, let's put these flowers in a vase. Nurse, could you help, please?"

Renee just lay propped on the pillows looking like someone who had come back from a long journey.

Her vital signs were good, her prognosis—said the doctor—was also good, although she would need rest for a few weeks just to be sure she was stable enough to return to normal life and activity.

She looked at Perry, but it was as if she were looking through him or past his shoulder at something. Perry continued to speak to her, fearing she might drift off and slip away again.

"Everybody at school will be so happy to see you, Renee. They all ask about you every day, and even the teachers have said they will help you get caught up in the work you've missed. And Mrs. Latimer had a baby boy named Patrick, and she brought him to school one day so everyone could see him and tickle his tiny feet."

So the afternoon passed into evening. They brought a tray of hospital food—the first meal Renee had eaten in nearly five weeks! It was soft food like pudding and oatmeal, but she ate it with appetite, which the nurse said meant her body was functioning properly.

When it was time to say 'goodbye' Perry let his tears fall on the pillow as he embraced Renee, smelling her hair and nuzzling her neck. Just like lovers, even though they weren't.

Renee lifted her head to Lisa and said two things: "Thank you" and "See you Saturday." Lisa Normal brushed a tear away and nodded.

All the way home Perry was silently thanking the Lord for His mercy, His profound Love for his family, and for Renee. Only God could have pulled this miracle off, he reminded himself. Only God could have answered his prayers.

That thought was a new one for Perry Normal, Junior Scientist, and it invited some thinking in a new direction. A spiritual one.

Chapter Eight   Expect The Unexpected

It was a full week after Renee came home that she could go out and about and go to The Malt Shop to meet the gang.

"Renee, wow. So good to see you."

"Good to be back. I guess it was touch and go for a while there."

"You could've died," said Robert awkwardly. "I mean, you had a close call, and we're all happy that you're okay."

"Perry suffered most of all," said Margot. "He is over the moon that you are back."

"Where is he?" asked Renee.

"Funeral for his grandparents," said Charmaine. "They were killed in a car crash about a week ago, I recall. Hit Perry hard."

"Perry has had a rough time lately, huh?" Max confirmed what everybody was thinking.

"I didn't know," said Renee. "He didn't say anything, and maybe that's best. I still feel a bit spaced out and not really myself, not like I was, if you know what I mean."

"Tell us more," said Robert.

"I had been pretty focused on intellectual pursuits like pure Science and Math.

But I feel like that 'me' has faded into the background and a new 'me' is emerging, taking charge of my life. And I don't really know who she is, at least not yet."

"Well, let us know when you find out," said Robert, good-naturedly.

"Let's eat," he said, pulling the fries and gravy plate that was supposed to be for everybody to share, close to his plate, where he off-loaded a fistful of fries.

"What was it like? Being in a coma?" Max was being his usual self, just blurting out whatever he was thinking about.

"Like being alive in another place."

"Like in a dream?" Charmaine asked.

"I guess. Only I couldn't wake up. Sometimes I felt like I needed to be somewhere else but I didn't know where or how to get there," Renee explained.

"Well, are you going to be alright? You're not going to fall back into unconscious-ness at some point, right?" Margot joined in.

"I don't think so, but like I said, I don't feel the same; my mind does things that I can't control or explain. I can still count from one to ten but I have a more holistic sense of what numbers mean, if you know what I mean."

"Whoa, big words you didn't use before, Renee," Robert said. "Holistic?"

"It means 'seeing the totality', the unity," said Margot. "And I kind of like the way you said that Renee. About what numbers *mean*, not just what they *do*. Numbers are a language and symbolize abstractions that may or may not have concrete applications."

"OMG!" said Charmaine. "It's catching! I don't think like this at all. It's like I'm having lunch with Einstein or Edison."

"Or Archimedes or Euclid," teased Robert. "Hey, where have the fries gone?"

"You ate most of them, greedy guts," Max said. "Let's order more; lots more."

***

Perry was almost invisible for the entire week. After the funeral, he stayed home for a day, alone in his room, alone with his thoughts.

So much had happened this year. He had lost his grandparents, almost lost his sweetheart. The world was full of disaster from hurricanes to earthquakes. Even his bike got stolen. All these losses were starting to take a toll on Perry.

He wanted 'alone-time' with Renee. She had to catch up on all the schoolwork she missed, of course. That meant long hours with teachers after school, and even longer hours in the library reading.

Perry tried to get her to come for a walk, or double with him on his bike. She seemed like she was not herself. She seemed a bit detached, distant, cool. There were too many questions in his mind and too few answers.

Finally he cornered her.

"Renee. I really need some time together. Please! You don't know what I've been through."

"Yes, Perry, I'm sorry. I'm still catching up—on everything. And there are things I want to say to you, but I don't know exactly *how*."

"Start, Renee. Start right now. Today. Come back to me. Come back to reality. Your nightmare is over."

Perry took her hands gently and firmly. He looked into those amber eyes, looked for the girl he knew. Was she still lost on that mountain in Vermont?

"Something happened, right at the beginning," Renee began.

"I didn't tell the doctors because I wasn't able to. And now it is irrelevant. But I want to tell *you*."

"I'm listening, Renee."

"The last thing I remember is being in the wind and shadow, sleet freezing my face and fingers. I don't remember hitting that tree, or wiping out.

I slipped out of my body. I must have because I was looking down at a crumpled girl in the snow, and wondering who she was, and why I was there with her."

"Go on."

"I felt very confused but it was getting very bright like the sun had come out and lit up the whole landscape. I looked up and felt drawn to the sun, to the light. And I floated somehow, that's how it felt—floating, or flying up. I didn't even think about where or why or about the girl in the snow anymore.

I felt wonderful, simply delighted that I was free somehow. Free of what I can't say but that feeling has remained in my mind, Perry."

As if to underline the experience, the sun came into the park from behind the new leaves and buds and shone directly down on the two friends on the bench.

"I wanted to fly forever in that light. And then I came to a bridge made of opal and alabaster—so many shifting colors, as if it were a living thing.

And I knew if I crossed it, I would not come back. It's so hard to explain. Like I was aware that I was here, and on the other side was another life, another reality. I knew I was completely free to choose. But something in me held back.

And then—nothing. Like it was a dream within a dream. The next thing I remember is someone calling my name, but I couldn't respond.

They were saying something else that didn't make any sense.

Someone said: 'Can you move your eyes?'. Well I thought *that* was strange. Of course I can move my eyes. I'm alive, aren't I? What kind of question was that?

And the very next thing I remember was waking up from sleep but I was in pain. My head hurt bad. I had a tube in my throat and nose, and my arm had a tube and it hurt too.

Then a nurse came and switched on a light and looked into my open eyes and said something I didn't understand either."

"What did the nurse say?" Perry asked.

"She said: "You've come back to us, Renee."

"I wondered how she knew my name and why was I lying in a hospital bed with all these tubes. Perry—it didn't feel like twenty-two days—it felt like a single, long night from which I had woken up."

Perry moved closer on the bench and put his arms around her tight.

"You *are* back, Renee. Everything will be alright now."

She pulled away a little so she could gaze into Perry's eyes.

"But I am different, Perry. Explain that! I see more colors around me, I sense movement, I feel that my awareness has expanded. Does this make any sense?"

"It *will*. Just give it time. I love you, Renee."

"You *do*?" But she smiled, and that made that green picnic area light up more than any sunbeam could.

***

The final submission dates for projects and assignments had arrived. Perry and Henry worked closely with Renee to ensure she finished the term work required. Somehow they had to condense a lot of material into a succinct form that she could absorb, otherwise she would not have a prayer of passing the exams.

The hard ones were Math and Science, not surprisingly. Luckily her two tutors were experts in both areas and Renee felt her confidence building as the hours of intense review and study went by. They all took the exams, and everyone—including Renee—

passed with flying colors. A long, drawn-out and dramatic year of school came to a close.

Yet Renee was different; she had changed. Her body was sitting in the booth in The Malt Shop but her spirit was drifting in rainbows and gossamer clouds.

"Any plans for the summer, Renee?" said Charmaine.

"I want to take some art classes, maybe learn to work in colors, paint my feelings," she said.

Charmaine looked at Rita and Margot.

"Sounds cool!" Charmaine replied.

"The art teacher Mrs. Ayers knows people who offer lessons," Rita said.

"Have you...I mean, are you...getting counseling, Renee?" Margot asked the thought on everyone's mind, but which no one dare say aloud.

"You think I'm crazy, don't you?" Renee shot back.

"No...no...not at all. But you did go through a rough time and maybe you don't wanna say how hard it has been coming back from...you know..."

"...the Dead?" Renee finished Margot's sentence. "I'm not a zombie or a vampire, you guys. I'm still Renee.

It's just that I...sense things, see things: colors nobody else can see, patterns in things. My hearing is much more acute. I hear birds singing and talking but I seem to understand what they are saying. I see rainbows in the sky, faint and kind of pastel pinks and greens and turquoise. But no, don't call me crazy. Call me..."

"Enhanced," said Robert sliding into the bench seat. "You've had a software upgrade," he said with confidence, waving at the waitress so he could order his usual.

Once the guys started to arrive, the girls changed the topic. Girl talk is for girls. Robert was loud and occasionally annoying, but he was a guy— and they are all like that.

"What's everybody doing for the summer?" chirped Max, sliding in to the booth across.

"Same old," said Charmaine. "Working at The Burger Palace takeout for ten bucks an hour."

"Burgers are important!" said Robert, ordering one with The Works and fries with gravy. Max ordered a cheeseburger and a Coke.

"I'm going to summer school to take Chemistry," said Margot. "Better to take it now than have it on top of all my courses in the Fall."

"Yuck," Max said. "What a waste of a long lazy summer. My folks may go on holiday and drag me along. Better than nothing."

"I'm going to look for a job," said Rita, "with my Uncle in the Bronx. He has a very busy Italian restaurant and needs help all the time. People don't want to work in the summer in New York so it's my opportunity to see the city!"

"The Big Apple!" Robert said between fries.

"Did they grow apples in New Amsterdam when the Dutch were there? Is that why it has that name?" Renee was curious.

"No. The name was given in the 1930s by somebody in New Orleans—which, by the way, is called The Big Easy. Anyhow, they saw New York City as this place of attraction and the name stuck. No apples. Ever."

"New York State is the biggest apple growing state, bigger than Washington," said Henry, coming in with Perry, seating themselves with Max.

"Then why don't we all get summer jobs picking apples?" asked Charmaine. "Then I don't have to work nights."

"Because the apples are not ready until October," replied Henry.

"What's up, Perry?" said Margot. "When do we get our final marks?"

"July fifteenth," said Perry. "I asked my Mom, who works for the School Board, how come we have to wait so long and she gave me some long-winded baloney that most administrators say to people, and which they actually believe."

And so the conversation went. The plates of food and glasses of root beer and Coke came and were consumed by the happy gang of Brackendale Middle School, in a place where Time stood still and the sun always shone.

CHAPTER NINE   FOR ALL I KNOW

It had been just over six months since the
accident. Everyone knew that. In a small tight group
like The Malt Shop gang, everyone was acutely aware
of what was going on in their respective lives, as if
they were one body and mind, an organism
composed of 7th graders, bound by a common destiny.

Rumors about Renee had begun circulating as
early as March, after she got out of the hospital, about
her remarkable new powers.

For instance, she predicted the wildfires that
started early in the Sierras and Pacific Northwest,
before the El Nino blocked the rains from coming,
leaving the forests tinder-dry and vulnerable to
lightning strikes. By June, hundreds of fires were
burning, and thousands of acres destroyed,
threatening homes and even towns, from Portland to
Santa Barbara.

She said earthquakes would signal that the
Yellowstone Park caldera was waking up, and sure
enough—geysers that were no more powerful than
fire hydrants blew steam and scalding water sky-high
-- which impressed the tourists but scared the Parks
Department and its geologists.

She predicted China would put a spacecraft on the Moon and begin a long process of exploration and establishment of a permanent Moon base. The nightly newscasts showed Chang E and Jade Rabbit crawling over the dusty grey surface, snapping remarkable pictures that were soon cut from live feed, due to their 'unusual' content.

"Can you tell me when I will get a boyfriend?" said Charmaine, over lunch at the diner.

Renee giggled. "I see...or rather, I *feel or sense* big stuff, global catastrophes and stuff like that. It's really hard to focus on something specific. I don't control it, this just comes to me."

"Try! Please!"

"Yeah, and after Charmaine, do me!" said Rita.

"She's not a fortune teller, people, so lighten up." Perry came to Renee's defense.

"I see an older guy, a big guy, he has a beard," said Renee. The group hushed up.

"He will really love you and protect you. He looks like a lumberjack or something."

"When?" interrupted Charmaine.

"Yeah, when?" said Rita and Margot.

"You will meet him at a picnic or outdoor event; a rodeo? Some kind of outdoor event. I'm getting it is summer cause it's hot and the trees are full of leaves, and there is smoke from a barbecue and lots of people and laughter."

"I'll check the papers," said Max. "They'll be advertisements for these kind of events and then we'll buy you a ticket!"

Everyone was chuckling, but deep down they were thinking: 'What if she turns out to be correct and Charmaine meets her dream-guy?'

"Me, next," said Rita.

"Hey, I was next," argued Max.

"Rita, you won't go to New York City, you will stay and graduate here." Renee was looking out the window at a place a million miles away judging by her expression.

"And Max, you will go to Chicago one day to attend university."

And so it went; each one of them getting a mini-psychic reading, until it was almost supper time.

Perry called 'time-out' when he saw that it was draining Renee.

***

"I'll walk you home," he said, taking her hand in the cool evening air.

"We really are trying to understand what's going on with you, Renee."

"I know, Perry. I just want people to treat me as normal, like I'm still me and I'm still one of the Brackendale gang and I am going to be okay, because honestly—I need to believe that more than anything."

In the moonlight filtering through the tall trees she looked ethereal, like a pale angel. That's how Perry would tell it later, when Renee was only a memory.

"You need to have a plan, for your summer, for your future, Renee. Keep focused on moving forward in your life. I heard you are going to study art, or painting—something like that. That sounds great!"

"I'm really looking forward to that. I've never tried painting before and there is a strong urge inside me to work with colors and shapes that I see in my mind. They mean something and even if nobody likes what I paint I feel something needs to come out, like I'm meant to speak in color, let my art say something."

Perry tightened his grip on her hand.

"I'm on a journey, Perry. I don't know how to say it. It's a journey I have to make alone."

"What do you mean—'alone'?" Perry paused and turned toward her, now lit by a streetlight.

"I've made a decision to return to Portland, after I finish packing. I have discussed this with my aunt and my mother and they agree that this would work. I'm leaving Brackendale, Perry, but I will never forget you."

She threw her arms around Perry's neck and pulled her body so tight to his that Perry could feel her heart beating. After a long embrace she let go, turned and walked into her aunt's house and closed the door without a glance backward.

* * *

"She left?" The girls were speaking to Perry all at once. "Why didn't you say something?"

"I couldn't. I mean I couldn't comprehend what was happening. She was walking with me and then—she…just… slipped away."

"What did you *say* to her?" Rita said.

"Nothing! Really! I told her that we were her friends for always. Especially me."

Perry looked down at his hands.

"You loved her didn't you?" said Charmaine.

"Yes, yes I guess I did. We went through a lot together," Perry admitted.

"I can't believe she did that!" said Rita. "Without telling us. Without *you* telling us."

"Lay off, Rita," Charmaine said. "You can see he's as messed up about it as we are."

"Sorry, Perry," Rita said. She reached across to take his hand. "She was your girl."

Perry never thought of it quite like that, but what Rita was saying was as close to the truth as Perry could admit to himself. Girl. Girlfriend. Friend. Caring. Now she was just....gone.

"Do you think she's going to be okay?" said Charmaine.

"I really don't know. She's become a bit strange since she came back. I kind of understand, but not really. Her personality has changed, her focus. Leaving so suddenly tells us that she was going through some deep stuff, dealing with her past and future all at once. Maybe that's why she had to go. I think it was more about her than it was her family -- trying to get her back on her feet."

"Does anyone have her email? I would hate for her to think we stopped thinking about her just because she up and left like that. Right?"

Rita was right about one thing. Renee Marchmount would not be forgotten and would be missed. There was a hole in their world, an empty spot on the bench in the booth where they all sat, day in and day out, sharing life, sharing fears and triumphs.

For Perry, it was a deep disappointment that was personal and upsetting. He had not gotten over the death of his grandparents and the abrupt departure of Renee touched that wound that all of us carry inside when a profound loss occurs.

The sun was not so warm or bright this June day and Perry went straight home to his room and locked the door, which was not like Perry at all.

CHAPTER TEN   THE END OF DAYS

The curious thing about prophecies is the frequency with which they actually come true. Perhaps Renee was good at extrapolation: reasoning from current, known conditions to future conditions. Perhaps any of us could predict severe weather or seismic activity if we studied the meteorological trends or reports of volcanic upswings in the Pacific Ring of Fire. But Renee was in recovery from a near-death experience that left her in a coma for weeks, and facing months—if not years—of rehabilitation. There was little to no possibility that she concocted a few lucky guesses about future events of a geographical nature. And certainly would not have done so to impress her small circle of friends.

Nevertheless upheavals and storms began to strike with such sudden ferocity that scientists and media specialists worldwide were caught by surprise. Powerful earthquakes in Mexico, in Chile, in Japan caused widespread panic and devastation. Massive floods—out of season—occurred in China and India, and also in central Europe, setting rainfall and river level records. Many called them '1000-year floods'.

The central and eastern United States experienced dramatic precipitation with tornadoes and freak windstorms, moving across the land like vengeful armies. Typhoons in the South Pacific Ocean ravaged small archipelago islands like Vanuatu -- which was leveled by sustained winds of 150mph. The Philippines received the bulk of the storm in the form of excessive rainfall and damaging winds that literally blew away villages and homes. To make matters worse, volcanoes on the islands started to spew steam and ash signaling a coming major eruption.

It was like the end of the world, and some doomsayers said as much in the media and on the Internet. Renee had told them this was to come soon. And she was right.

Perry was watching the six-o'clock news with his father, Robert.

"Authorities are monitoring the situation closely tonight..."said the broadcaster. Lurid pictures of survivors huddled in the rain under tarps and makeshift tents, with no shoes or jackets gave emphasis to the havoc these events were causing.

"Thousands are without power at this hour, hampering rescue efforts and adding to the loss of life," the news announcer went on.

It didn't matter whether it was Manila or Melbourne or Miami—planet-wide disaster was in full swing.

"Why aren't the governments prepared, Dad?" Perry turned to his father who had his feet up and was reading Time magazine and sipping his decaf.

"Many countries don't have the infrastructure in place, Perry, and that is for several reasons. First off, disaster preparedness is not a priority if your economy is struggling to begin with. Second, the coordination between central and local governments is often sadly lacking. I guess what I'm saying is that government bureaucracy is often the people's worst enemy and times of trouble expose its hidden weakness."

"We've got emergency response all planned out in the U.S., right? So no matter what Mother Nature throws at us, we'll be ready huh Dad?"

"Well we're certainly in a better position that most Third World nations and we can be assured that our tax dollars are being used to have plans and personnel in place if the worst happens."

Perry secretly wondered what his father meant by 'the worst'; he headed upstairs to his computer to do some quick research into what kind of disasters historically had been experienced in the United States. He also pinged his best friend Henry on Gtalk so he could exchange ideas and chitchat.

* * *

"Hey, Perry. I just got a brilliant idea. There is a Science Symposium in August at Cornell and I really want to go. What if we put together a short presentation on global disasters or disasters that could happen in the United States and present it under the Student category? That would be wicked! We could get a certificate or something that might earn us a credit in Science next year."

"I'm into that Henry. Who better to do it than junior scientists with an excellent track record? We got written up for our adventures in Florida and the relics from Atlantis we donated to the museum. The public likes that stuff!"

"Totally! I know lots of people want to know why this year is particularly bad for various disasters—we could, like, do a multi-part presentation on each type: earthquakes, volcanoes, hurricanes. We could hopefully get it done by the deadline."

"Okay. Let's have a serious meeting about this, Henry, at a prestigious local venue for discussing such scholarly issues: The Malt Shop. At three."

"I'll be there," Henry replied. "They have a new vegan burger that sounds gross but I want to try it."

"Later, my friend."

* * *

Perry and Henry huddled together at the rear of the restaurant.

"The obvious place to start is with tectonics: earthquakes, volcanoes, and why they are happening more and more," said Perry.

"Agreed," Henry said. "And how much of a real danger they represent to civilian populations. Like in Seattle, or San Francisco. And don't forget tsunamis."

"Then, we can tackle bigger issues like the Campi Flegrei in Naples or the Yellowstone Caldera. People are talking, people are concerned. Millions would die if either of these 'supervolcanoes' erupts suddenly!"

"Do you know NASA has a plan in place to cool down Yellowstone, Perry?"

"I heard about it but I want to see the details; it sounds crazy but the government must know the danger is real, so the response must be ready. Hard to believe things like this are even possible."

Perry took a sip from his vanilla milkshake.

"And what about global climate chaos, Henry? That one is causing far more damage and disruption to commerce and agriculture. Could we do part of our report on that?"

"I think we should but there are no firm theories we can rely upon; we would be out in left field with our hypotheses. I mean, that never stopped us before, but we don't want to alarm people or let them think we are a couple of nutcases. We need proof, Perry."

"Wait a second, Henry—I think you hit the nail on the head. We are scientists and scientists offer evidence, if not outright proof. What if we compare and contrast prophecy—which is intuitive guesswork, or whatever—with real science. Science predicts with a sound foundation of fact. Psychic prophecies are the product of wild imaginings or coincidence...no offence to Renee."

"Awesome, Perry! That is perfect! The public is spooked and is looking for answers. We can offer the comfort of scientific reasoning, which brings us closer to reality. Let's get started, shall we?"

And so the two boys launched their newest adventure in Science – making Earth changes comprehensible for ordinary people.

* * *

"Okay, let's put a framework together for this, Henry."

Perry Normal was outstanding at organizing information and adapting it for public presentation. He proved it at the Science Fair where his time-travel presentation won first prize. He proved it again in Florida when he defended the notion that Atlantis might well have existed off the coast of America.

"Okay, Henry. Let's divide it into two parts: one dealing with geological events, and one dealing with meteorological events. We break down each category into three topics using the headings 'What', 'How', and 'Why'. What is this phenomenon about, How does it affect the population of a specific location, and Why is it happening *now*?"

"Sounds great, Perry. But how do we avoid duplicating our efforts if we both work on the same topic?"

"We don't. You will do the volcanic and seismic part, since that is your expertise anyhow and I will do the more difficult to explain the part on climate change. Then we stitch it together and see what we've got."

"That sounds great. I know just where I want to begin. I will start with something dramatic, with statistics that show how perilous the situation is globally, and particularly for the United States. Hawaii is under serious threat from Kilauea with over 500 quakes a day breaking the crust to let red lava spew out. It's on the news; it's relevant."

"You are so clever, my boy! I'm going home to have dinner and I will text you later. I have some ideas of my own that I need to get on paper."

* * *

"Hey Perry." His dad called him into the living room. "Look at what is going on. NBC is having a TV special next week on the new FEMA camps being built all over the country with housing for hundreds of people and heavy security."

"What's going on with that Dad?"

"I have no idea. First I've heard of it. Are they expecting a disaster on a national scale? An invasion? I really don't know."

"Okay, let's tape it. I've got something to do so I'm going to my room. Talk to you later Dad."

Perry had to gather his thoughts. *What are the current explanations for climate change? Global warming caused by human industrial pollution. We may be past the tipping point, and we cannot get control of atmospheric conditions.*

What about global cooling? The British MET office declared that we are moving into a new ice age. Seriously? Perry wanted to see the science behind that statement. *How can we have global warming and global cooling at the same time?* This seemed contradictory and illogical, yet there was evidence that this is exactly what is going on.

Perry began to consider the possibility that climate change on Earth might be related to cosmic explanations, some of which had become popular as global weather took a turn for the worse.

Perry was texting.

"Henry! Could it be that the Sun is causing all this? We both know that the Sun drives the ocean circulation and global wind patterns but the Sun is going into a solar minimum cycle and that must surely affect our planet?"

"True," Henry texted back. "Low sunspot activity, absence of coronal flares resulting in diminished radiant heat."

"Lemme go back to my notes. There's got to be a cause that we are not looking at clearly. Maybe something unknown. From Space, I mean."

Somebody had posted a video on YouTube suggesting that the Earth's axis was shifting or had already tilted several degrees. If that were true we would see unusual weather because the solar warming would occur differently and some places would be cooler and some hotter.

The United States was experiencing hotter temperatures than ever recorded before. California was in a pernicious drought. But Canada and the Northeast had a bitter cold winter with temperatures similar to the North Pole! None of it made sense.

Some news reports suggested that the sun came up in a different direction and daylight lasted longer than is typical for this time of year. But that is not necessarily proof of an axis shift. It's what they call 'anecdotal evidence'-- reports by people who experience unusual events that frighten or confuse them. "A scientist cannot afford to be confused." Mr. Matson, the Science teacher, once said to him. Some of the best advice Perry would ever get. But still...

"Henry. What if it is cyclical?" Perry was texting his friend again.

"You mean every few years this kind of stuff happens to the weather—like El Nino, you mean?"

"Exactly. Like El Nino. Nobody knew about this strange oscillation in the Pacific Ocean currents off the Equator until someone hypothesized that the change in ocean temperature could affect the climate of both North and South America in a big way. It was the El Nino of 1973 that really gave that idea some traction," Perry said.

"So a number of seemingly unrelated factors could be overlapping and causing unpredictable and violent weather phenomena?"

"Yeah, man! That is what I'm saying here!"

"Well write all that down Perry, before you forget it!"

"No probs. I will jot that into my notes. Can I text you even if it's late Henry?"

"Of course. I never power off."

"Thanks, Henry. You are my sounding board. You are the only one I can really talk to."

"Keep me posted Einstein!"

The last thought Perry had before turning out the lights was a flashback to what happened last summer when he was a guest at JPL in Pasadena. He had some evidence that Planet X, or Planet 9 as NASA called it, was real and was moving closer to our solar system, or maybe was even inside the Kuyper Belt.

That would explain why several planets were heating up, according to astronomers. That would explain how Earth's axis might be pulled out of line by the gravity of some giant celestial body. People were hotly debating whether it could be a rogue planet, a brown dwarf star, or huge comet. The military indicated to Perry that he should not worry about such things and to use his telescope for more mundane purposes.

But, what if...? That was his last thought until he woke up early the next morning, and could hear his dad making coffee downstairs, and letting the cat out.

* * *

Perry and Henry were at The Malt Shop. Robert and Max were also there, since the food was always fresh, tasty, and cheap.

'Food is a man's best friend', Robert liked to say. The owner Dave was very fond of the Brackendale gang Dave often told them, and who comprised 30% of his customer base.

"What's doing, Perry?" said Robert. "You have that intense expression you get when you are working on a project."

"You are right, Robert. Henry and I are putting together a discussion on the scientific basis for global upheaval."

"Oh, *that!*" Robert said mockingly. "Max and I were discussed the baseball season's prospects for the Yankees. Minor, compared to what you guys are doing."

Everyone laughed. Then they tucked into a hefty meal of burgers, fries, and shakes.

Charmaine and Rita arrived, ordered, and joined them in pigging out on diner fare.

"Have you...has she..." Charmaine said to Perry.

"Actually, no," said Perry. "I have no idea what's going on with Renee."

"Don't worry. When she's ready, she'll talk. Just let her alone for now."

"What choice do I have?" said Perry bitterly.

"Hey, have you guys heard about the FEMA recruitment going on in upper New York?" Rita was speaking now.

"What?" said Max and Robert at the same time.

"FEMA—the Federal Emergency Management Agency—is hiring summer students for twelve bucks and hour to train for local emergency response in case of...".

"In case of what?" Robert asked.

"In case the shit hits the fan," said Max, half-jokingly.

"I dunno, check the website. I don't want to spend this summer waitressing so I might sign up," Rita said. "And anyhow, I'm not going to New York after all, I've decided."

"There have been at least seventeen near-misses by asteroids so far this year," said Henry, matter-of-factly.

"Great," said Robert. "That will have an impact on the Yankees' chances of getting into the World Series."

"Ha ha, great pun, Robert: 'impact' the Yankees' chances...of course an asteroid or meteor is going to have some impact, particularly if it lands near *us!*" Max said.

"Hey, want me to show you a new card game, people? It's called 'euchre'. My auntie plays it with her friends and taught it to me last weekend." Charmaine dug out a deck of cards and began to shuffle.

"Perfect for our little group," she continued.

"...who are seriously bored and in need of a life," said Robert.

Perry and Henry excused themselves muttering something about The End of Days and the coming catastrophe, which fell on deaf ears anyway.

"Watch the TV special tonight at eight, Henry. My Dad and I are going to. Hey! Why don't you come over to our house? I'll ask my Mom if you can stay for dinner."

Once all the consents were obtained, Henry and Perry and Mr. Normal sat waiting for the commercials to end, and the program to begin.

'This is a special presentation about federal emergency planning that will affect the lives of all Americans,' the TV announcer announced.

Millions of Americans were glued to the tube this evening to watch this unusual show, that had been hyped in all the media. 'Why was it such a big deal?' people wondered.

Taverns and sports bar changed the channel just to have it on.

State officials and law enforcement had the channel tuned to NBC as well.

Something was up.

CHAPTER ELEVEN   BE PREPARED

For some reason, the federal government was preparing America for an unknown, unspecified emergency situation.

Hundreds of National Guards and army personnel were joining forces in each of the ten designated areas that formed the new map of the United States, a FEMA map that showed different regions assigned a number and given an overseeing military authority.

Soldiers were deployed in an exercise called Operation Jade Helm, to protect society against social disorder in the event of an emergency.

FEMA had set up camps to provide food, shelter, clothing, and medical care for victims and civilians who had been displaced from their communities.

But the government was strangely quiet about what would cause such disorder and chaos in a country of established law and order, where the Constitution gave every citizen rights and liberty under the umbrella of democracy.

Perry and Henry were whispering frantically to each other on the couch.

"This relates to what our project is about," said Henry.

"You think they know something big is going to happen?" said Perry, leaning close to Henry's ear.

"Well something is!" said Henry. "That's plain as day."

Then the program broke for a commercial; this was about what Rita had mentioned in the diner.

FEMA was recruiting youth participants who would be trained (and paid) for six weeks training, in locations scattered across New York and Ohio. There was a website and toll-free phone number to call so Perry jotted it down.

After normal programming resumed and the nightly news came on, Perry excused himself to walk Henry home.

"There's only one way to find out what is really going on Perry," said Henry.

"I know what you are going to say, Henry."

"Well, why not? Ask your parents; I'll ask mine."

"Alright. I'll talk to you later online. This is going to be cool!" But Perry secretly wondered what he was getting himself into.

* * *

It turned out that a shuttle bus from Newton Ave. near the Malt Shop picked up those who had registered for the FEMA Boot Camp which was situated a ways out of town. The facility had Quonset huts including a cafeteria, medical station, offices, a shooting range, and training grounds. In fact, it was a decommissioned military site not used since the end of the Cold War, but now was humming with activity and vehicles of various kinds.

"Do we get uniforms?" Henry was so excited that he began his usual jabbering non-stop.

There were some familiar faces: Charmaine, Rita, Margot and Max had all signed up; kids from nearby schools including private schools had enrolled. One boy who had been expelled for drugs was there because his probation officer said it would look good and keep him on the straight and narrow.

Altogether there were about fifty-five recruits under twenty and an equal number of older adults, some even retired, such as former police officer Carl Lindt who was a state trooper for many years.

Perry and Henry had both discussed the curriculum -- which included firearms training and some pretty grueling field exercises, not unlike what the army gives you -- with their parents.

"When do we get to shoot the guns?" Henry continued to blabber.

"Hey, Rita, hey Charmaine, hey Margot!" Perry hugged his friends and shook Max' hand.

"You ready for all this?" he said.

"Worth a try," said Charmaine. "I need to lose five pounds anyway."

"Why do we have to do push-ups?" Henry was forlorn.

But day by day, the whole cohort started to get into shape, running, jumping, climbing, all of which later turned out to be basic survival skills.

Fitness training was just the beginning. Survival and emergency preparedness was a lot of things that ordinary folk should be aware of. Home and self-defense would come much later in the program. Henry's new relationship to firearms would have to wait.

* * *

The army instructor was explaining what events might cause the familiar infrastructure to collapse. He said roads and bridges would be out, highways clogged with families trying to drive away and escape, the electrical grid system would probably be down, and the streets and plazas and houses plunged into darkness.

This could be caused by storms, floods, quakes, criminal or terrorist activity. The purpose of this summer 'camp' was to learn how to respond in small groups within the community.

"What will you eat when the stores are all closed?" The sergeant was surveying the recruits seated on the ground, the morning sun coming up hot and the humidity building.

"We've got a freezer full of food," offered one gentleman who was bald and sweating.

"Wrong," said the sergeant. "With no power for days, everything would have melted or spoiled in the first week."

"Then we could have a huge barbecue!" said some young guy back in the fourth row.

"Then those families without food would arrive uninvited, so you would have to consider whether you have enough wings or burgers for all them, too!" the sergeant said.

"What I want to cover today is how to forage for food in the wild so to speak. There are plants, roots, berries that are edible, and found in local parks and ravines. We will focus on these easily harvested greens first, before we get into trapping squirrels, pigeons, snakes, and other common animal sources of nutrition."

"Snakes?" said Rita.

"You've got to be kidding me!" said Charmaine.

"Taste like chicken, my uncle says," said Max.

"I wouldn't know," said Henry. "I prefer steak."

All his friends laughed, but suddenly quieted down as the sergeant gave them instructions.

"We won't bivouac, tonight, but tomorrow we will learn to build primitive shelter such as a lean-to and sleep in the Great Outdoors. I hope you all brought your sleeping bag and pillows, as the registration instructions were quite clear."

"I'm putting you into teams, called squads, five people on a squad, with one leader who will translate my orders into action for your squad. So get yourself into groups of six now, pick your captain and send them to me in the hut over there for briefing on the mission of the day."

One hundred and ten people jumped to their feet and, in the commotion, managed to sort themselves as commanded, and began to discuss the material handed out by the sergeant.

Each squad was assigned a code number, like A-1, A-2, B-1, and so on. But the fun part was choosing a moniker for each squad, like The Ragged Boys, or The Z-Team. They began to function as a unit, which, of course, was the goal. That's military training and it works.

"What do we do next?" said Rita.

"We have to find five different plants from this list, that are edible raw or steamed. Let's start with dandelions," Perry said.

Perry was their leader, naturally, and they were 'The Malt Shop Gang', which was no surprise to anyone. Other groups thought the name was funny but it meant a lot to some homesick kids from Brackendale, New York.

The chatter began to subside as the day got warmer and the squads all got down to the task of actually studying the plants and shrubs that they had failed to notice in regular life.

Perry knew that many edibles could be found in damp areas, by brooks or creeks. Since they needed one more item to complete their assignment, Perry stepped on a stone in the stream and pointed.

"Behold! The stinging nettle! Painful to touch, but nutritious and full of vitamins."

"Who gets to have the honor of pricking their hands to collect it?" said Max.

"Let's draw straws," said Henry. "Like in the survival movies!"

"A better question is 'who has a knife?'" said Perry.

Henry took out his folding Swiss knife and passed it to Perry. Perry deftly cut the slender branches, and folded them into a wad of birch bark, allowing him to escape the sting from tiny hairs lining the fronds.

Each squad submitted their list, initialed by their captains, and were checked off by the sergeant, who—to everyone's relief—shouted: "Lunch time!" and clumps of hot and tired recruits stampeded into the outdoor mess hall and lined up for hot food and cold drinks.

"This chili is a little bit more spicy than I'm used to," said Rita, "but it is really good!"

"At least they didn't skip on the ground beef," said Max. "Too bad Robert isn't here; he would love this stuff."

After lunch, the sergeant was kind enough to let them sit under a shady roof in an outdoor tent that seemed half the size of a football field.

"Imagine you have no gun, only a knife at most, and you have to find meat; the reality is you could survive as a vegetarian for awhile but your body needs protein and the easiest way to get it is animal food," he said.

The sergeant had a projector and a laptop and was showing a Powerpoint with pictures of typical targets:

rodents and fish. Rita was glad he didn't go back to discussing snakes.

"Squirrels and rabbits are found in abundance. Woodchucks and mice can be found too. Use a snare made of thin wire on the path they take—they won't see it but you have to move in for the kill quickly."

One lady said: "How do we kill it?" followed by murmurs from the crowd that we get our food in the supermarkets and it's already dead.

"Good point. Turn the axe head to the flat side and strike the animal's head with a strong blow or two. Or use a handy rock. Remember—this is an emergency and you have to eat, so it's no time to be squeamish. It's not a cute little bunny! It's dinner!"

Charmaine looked at Rita and mimicked: 'It's not a cute little bunny—it's dinner.'

Max smiled and Henry rubbed his forehead.

"Now, if you are lucky and have a stream or lake nearby, fish is the ideal menu item."

The sergeant showed how to build a simple weir in a stream where fish would be trapped and easily taken, and how to make a simple hook and line—with or without a rod—that would bring in the catch of the day.

Then they went out into the grounds and practiced making fire. Most used matches or cigarette lighters but the tinder had to be all natural materials like dry twigs, or seed pods.

Perry impressed everyone by using the birch bark he had collected since it contains flammable resins that burn hot once it gets started.

They learned how to build a scaffolding type campfire -- with lots of ventilation for the fire to burn into coals that could be used to bake or boil whatever food had been gathered.

"Why didn't we join Boy Scouts, Perry?" asked Henry.

"Too busy learning the Periodic Table, I guess."

"Do you know that Boy Scouts of America now accepts girls?" said Charmaine.

"It's about time," Perry remarked.

"When's dinner?" said Max.

As if on cue, the dinner bell rang just like it did in the cowboy days in trail camps -- only now it was software connected to speakers.

Sitting next to Charmaine at the table was a husky young man in a lumberjack shirt. His beard was tinged red and he seemed to be at least twenty. He introduced himself as Kirk and all through dinner spent most of his time chatting with Charmaine. She was very drawn to this boy and they promised to connect on social media after this army adventure was over.

Outside of any town or city one is struck by the incredible numbers of stars at night, a glittering sea of crystal cast across the heavens, as if to remind human beings that they are but a small part in a vast Creation.

So The Malt Shop gang sat quietly around a small campfire, poking the smoldering sticks into the center, watching it flame up and send sparks up toward those distant stars, themselves giant furnaces of cosmic fire shining eternally in the dark depths of Space.

* * *

Days began to turn into weeks. Routine was the order of the day in the military and was impressed on all the participants. Up at 7:00am, wash and eat, report for duty at 8:30. Train all day, eat at 6:00, lights out by 10:00.

The training this week, Week Two, was all about first aid procedures, and how to assist the injured. Some participants had done basic First Aid at work but for some it was a revelation: how to stop bleeding; how to restore breathing and consciousness; how to treat a burn. Every single one of them knew they would need to use this one day. It was a certainty.

Perry showed his squad how to use a triangular bandage to support a broken arm. What he also taught them—and the first aid manual did not mention—is that it works well for a broken collarbone.

"How do you break your collarbone?" said Max.

"You fall, and try to break the fall with your arm. In the old days falling off a horse was a common way. But I see skateboarders take falls and don't even know they've broken a bone. So, watch it again; especially getting the knot in the right place, behind the neck on the side of the break."

On Friday, in the presentation tent, the sergeant then reviewed situations like earthquakes or landslides that cause structures to collapse and severe injuries to the occupants.

He even used real video footage of quakes in Japan and Turkey to emphasize the scale of damage. He also showed the Northridge Quake in Los Angeles and the damage to highways and apartment buildings.

Then he dropped a bombshell—the mayor of Los Angeles admitted, to the media, that the city does not have adequate resources to deal with another, perhaps larger, quake. They don't have the funds, they don't have enough firefighters or police or even hospitals to handle mass casualties, or fires, or to handle a deadly tsunami racing in from the Pacific and taking out coastal communities like Santa Monica or Venice.

"What this means, folks, is that we are going to be on our own out there. And all the survival skills you ever learned will now decide who lives and who dies."

The seated crowd was quiet and thinking about New York City, and Atlanta, and Honolulu, and San Francisco, and just about any coastal town that came to mind, especially those where family might live, where holidays might be spent.

"Next week, we are going to train you in the safe and proper use of firearms and also basic self-defense without weapons because there will be lawlessness for a time during and after a disaster,and without police or army protection, you have to handle it yourselves."

"Bang, bang!" said Max.

"Bang, bang," echoed Henry, obviously excited.

"Ooooh, martial arts," said Charmaine. "I'm gonna kick your pimply butt, Max!" She started to chase him across the field, whacking him with a stick.

Perry said, "I wonder why they want citizens to know all this all of a sudden. Earthquakes drills, self-defense, use of weapons. What do they expect is going to happen?"

"Maybe they will tell us in the final week," said Henry.

"Or just let the chips fall," said Perry with a somber tone of voice.

He picked up his cellphone and texted to his mom that everything was fine, and they were learning lots of neat stuff about survival. But still, that nagging question hung in his mind.

Why are we learning all this?

* * *

The final ten days of training would be what-if scenarios. Some of the squads would be responding to a weather event, like a hurricane, which was funny because hurricane season had already started in Florida and some pretty nasty storms were making landfall.

Other squads did earthquake drills, like the ones schoolchildren in Seattle were practicing—only the exercise involved managing wounded, setting up emergency shelter, and protecting people or sites against looters or attack. It was a comprehensive exercise to demonstrate competence at putting survival skills to the test. And the sergeant became a stern taskmaster. He did not tolerate ignorance, sloppy technique, or lazy attitudes.

Three groups had a special assignment: disease outbreak or epidemic. This called for special attention to the unique dangers of contagion, what to do with casualties and with the corpses of victims. A specialist from the Center for Disease Control in

Atlanta was brought in to brief them and supervise the exercise.

Several teams were constructing shelters using tarps and plastic sheeting. Some were digging latrines -- an often overlooked requirement of any kind of camp. Some were organizing soup kitchens using minimal equipment and various types of dried or canned food. Some were training to use fire extinguishers or set-up bucket brigades to suppress fires that would spread in camps with wooden structures.

Perry's team got to be medics. They bandaged, set up cots, learned to prioritize the serious cases, and what to do with scanty medical supplies -- especially medications and painkillers.

Nurses came in to show them how an IV is set up, how to monitor vital signs and symptoms, and how to communicate with any doctors who might be available to help. They did not expect to do blood or urine tests; this was not business as usual -- this was day-to-day survival until normal social functioning was restored. This included electrical power, water and heat: those fragile linkages that keep us alive and healthy.

The interesting thing was that individual teams could circulate and observe activities of the other squads -- provided they did not get in the way. Thus almost everyone got to see how emergencies of every conceivable kind were managed.

Henry had learned to eat wild plants—but no rabbits; he had learned how to shoot a standard Army issue rifle from a standing and supine position, and he had learned how to make a tourniquet for a severe bleeding limb. He had learned that pushups build your chest muscles -- allowing you to carry and move heavy stuff better. His confidence in his own abilities had emerged from six grueling weeks of training. He told his friends he was considering joining the National Guard.

"Is this the Henry we know and love?" quipped Charmaine. But her eyes showed respect for Henry's accomplishments.

All of the members of the Malt Shop Gang had grown in important ways, ways that only they knew, and shared. They were strong now. They were prepared.

On the bus ride back home they chatted and laughed and joked that they got paid to do all this -- which was even better. None of them could have guessed that sooner than they would have ever expected this training would be put to the test.

ACT III   HOW IS A BUTTERFLY BORN?

CHAPTER TWELVE   DUST IN THE WIND

The news was bad. Very bad. A massive storm with devastating winds had swept into Ohio and Western New York. Rainfall quickly caused every stream and river to rise to perilous levels—record levels in many cases.

In its wake came tornadoes, uncommon in the Great Lakes region, catching the towns and cities unprepared and soon—without electrical power.

People don't realize how dependent we are on electricity. Hospitals, offices and government facilities such as fire and police stations, traffic lights. All out of service. Cell towers down and every electronic device now with failing battery power. Gas stations were unable to operate pumps, so fuel was no longer available.

The call to every emergency volunteer went out nevertheless, over social media and television, radio, Internet: the Governor was declaring a 'state of emergency' in Ohio, Indiana, and New York. This meant two things: each state could call for federal aid, such as FEMA and the National Guard, and each state was in a desperate situation that would put every citizen and business on alert for impending danger.

Henry got a text first; then Perry. Then Max and Rita and Charmaine, and dozens more who had participated in the summer training. Their little squad met at The Malt Shop, which was running on a generator to provide light and enough power to make coffee and snacks.

"My parents don't want me to go out in this," said Charmaine.

"Isn't this what we trained for?" said Rita.

"Yeah, but not to just jump in and get ourselves killed!" Max was serious.

"What do everybody's parents say?" said Perry.

"Mine don't really approve," said Henry. "'Let the pros take charge', they said."

"Yeah! We are just kids, after all," Rita spoke up and Max nodded vigorously.

"We may not have a choice," said Perry. "We are among the few who can actually help and there must be situations that the fire department and police department can't respond to."

"So what do you suggest?" said Charmaine.

"Me, personally, I would start with the home for the elderly or the hospital. That's where we're going to find the most vulnerable, most dependent individuals."

"What about the daycare and kindergarten and primary schools?" Henry said. "We don't even know if the children made it home and with the streets either flooded or wires and trees down, parents must be frantic to reach their kids. I think the police have higher priorities right now and cannot render assistance."

"Oh, you said that like a real rescue person," said Rita, throwing an arm around Henry's neck. "Be my hero, Henry?" she teased.

"Get in line," Margot joked.

"I've still got 40% on my i-Phone," said Perry. "Let me call the local Emergency Response number and see if I can get anyone."

Someone picked up; Perry identified himself and the reason for his call.

"They said come to the headquarters if we are able to travel and we will be assigned tasks assisting authorities who are working search and rescue missions, or sandbagging river banks, or assisting people who are trapped in their homes and may be injured."

"This is it, guys," said Perry. "If you want to come with me that would be great. If you feel you can't make it I totally understand. Go home and take care of your family."

It was awkward; the moment of decision that training had not exactly told them they would have to face. The emotional dimension of disaster. The test of courage.

"I will do it if everyone agrees to stick together," said Henry.

"OK Perry, we're in—let's get it done," said Charmaine. She used Perry's cell to text her mom to hold dinner—she was going to be late.

* * *

The mile-and-a-half trip to the rescue facility was an adventure all on its own.

The water in the street was ankle deep and branches and debris from buildings were strewn across sidewalks. Cars were just left abandoned on the roadside and trash was blowing sideways. And the worst was that it was now completely dark.

Henry tripped on a telephone wire that was hung up on a fence and could not be seen.

He was startled but not hurt.

They trudged on until the bright lights from the generators revealed the presence of a group milling about near the facility they were reporting to.

Guardsmen were there in jeeps and trucks, sorting tools and equipment.

Once inside, The Malt Shop Gang was directed to the commander who was a military officer. They were signed in.

"Sir? We are a squad from Camp Seneca and if possible, we really want to stay together as a unit. We trained as a unit and we can serve as a unit."

"Very well, uh, Perry, is it?"

"Yes, sir!"

"Okay, we have a rescue squad heading out to Malvern Road where we have a stranded school bus trapped under a collapsed cell tower. Know any first aid?"

"We do, sir."

"Good! Go with Lieutenant Grant over there—the tall skinny guy—and tell him he's responsible for your safe deployment and return. Any questions?"

"No sir!" Perry replied crisply, as he felt the urgency of the rescue mission.

Max said to Perry when they had a moment: "Do you think we will get paid?"

Henry snorted. "You'll be lucky to not get killed Max, you moron." Henry was pumped and tied his bootlaces with a double knot.

He was especially excited that their vehicle was a Humvee, the best four-wheel drive vehicle the army had. It also had heat which the girls especially appreciated. A combination of sweat and damp from rainfall can chill the body quickly to a state of dangerous hypothermia. The only cure was keep eating high calorie snacks and shielding yourself from the wind.

They were lucky. The roads were passable and they found the bus upright but crumpled from the weight of thousands of pounds of steel framework and cable. When the headlights of the Humvee shone on the windows, children started yelling and crying.

First out were the electrical guys: they had to determine if there was a live wire touching any of the metal -- which would instantly electrocute anyone careless enough to make contact.

"All clear, Lieutenant."

They scrambled out and were told that, once the wreckage of the tower was removed, they were to go in and bring the kids out, one at a time.

"How they gonna do that?" said Max.

"Wait," said Perry. "They have a welder moving tanks into position. He's going to cut the metal away, so it can free up the front door and maybe pop the windshield out."

Sure enough, white hot sparks started to fly into the mist that hung over the hills of Brackendale. First one piece of metal was cut through and pulled away by a soldier, then another, and another.

"We're in, Lieutenant. The driver is dead."

"Dead?" whispered Rita. "We didn't train to deal with dead people."

"They've got him, Rita. Once he's out we go in. Those kids are going to be totally freaked so let's have a huddle and get a plan together."

Perry got a 6-volt lantern flashlight and stood at the rear exit door. He pried it open from the outside, standing on a crate but once it was open he and Max placed two 2x12 planks up to the opening. Max nailed a strip of plywood near the top and in the middle to stabilize them. It was time to go in. Each one of The Malt Shop Gang realized children's lives were hanging in the balance, as they heard groans and cries from the dark cavern within.

Charmaine ran up the gangplank to everyone's surprise. Her voice could be heard, reassuring and firm, as if she had done this a thousand times.

"Perry! We need blankets or towels or something here!"

Rita and Max scurried over to the Humvee and lifted supplies out of a metal cabinet on the side of the vehicle.

"Oh Jesus. Perry. I have a casualty here." Charmaine said. "He's dead."

"Leave him. Get the others. I'm coming in."

One by one the intrepid troop of 7th Graders, who were still kids themselves, pulled, lifted, and hauled 3rd Graders from the metal coffin out onto stretchers or tarps laid on the earth.

Altogether eighteen youngsters were removed—not including the two who had succumbed to cold and injury. Rita and Charmaine, mainly, were giving first aid to those who had cuts from broken glass or broken arms or ribs from the violent impact that brought their usual ride home to a sudden and frightening ending.

The Lieutenant had radioed in for an ambulance that was a modified school bus itself—meant for mass evacuation, and fitted out with beds and medical supplies to treat victims. All the surviving children were secured in the vehicle, seat belts fastened, blankets draped over their small, shivering bodies.

The squad followed the bus back to town, then veered off to HQ for a much-needed break and something to eat.

"Well, now we know what dead people look like," said Max.

"I wonder what they'll have us do next?" said Henry. "I hope it's not filling and hefting sandbags down by the creek!"

"Hey! We'll volunteer Henry for that," Max quipped.

The Lieutenant came up and sat down on the bench, momentarily relieved to be sipping a steaming coffee.

"You did well, Team," he said with a smile that made all of them feel warm inside.

"Can you handle one more tonight?"

"Yes, sir," Perry said -- knowing his gang was right beside him.

"The volunteers at the community center have opened up the two gymnasiums for folks whose homes are not safe and have nowhere to go tonight. They need more warm bodies to help them prepare and serve hot food, arrange sleeping areas and bedding for about a hundred and twenty people, most of them families. They will be tired and discouraged and the children especially will need support getting settled down. Are you up for it?"

"How do we get over to the center?" Perry asked.

"The Humvee will run you over there. I am needed here, but Sergeant Filion will handle the logistics on this one. Thanks again you guys. You have no idea how much you are needed right now. I know you would prefer to be home in bed but you can be sure you are making a material difference to the citizens of Brackendale!"

Psychologists will tell you that people are motivated by positive reinforcement and the best way to inspire people to give it everything they've got is to praise them. The Lieutenant's candid statement was like whiskey in their veins! They piled into the Hummer like an elite army unit.

The community center had big ceiling lights running and the whole scene was like a movie set: people running around, a constant swell of sound from a hundred human voices rising and falling as they filled the large interior space.

Since they had been issued armbands signifying they were FEMA-authorized workers, they found they could move around easily as people --their eyes hopeful and grateful --moved out of their way, and they each took a station and began ushering people to the place they needed to be right now.

Most of the people sat on the floor so blankets and mats were laid out. There were even a few cribs for the babies. Rita and Charmaine decided they should help the new mothers and parents with their children, fetching food, blankets, pillows, even toys.

A group of older men lingered just outside the doors -- smoking and talking in low voices.

Perry and Henry were security detail --making sure that anyone who entered was legitimately there; they had been told that looters and pickpockets were often present in times of emergency. They also directed people to washrooms where faucets and toilets were operating normally and one area off the big gym had showers but no hot water.

Max got pulled into the kitchen detail: washing pots and pans and dishes by having kettles warm up water on a propane stove and then mixing it with cold tap water in the big sinks in the kitchen behind the gym. One of the guidance counselors from school recognized him and insisted he was indeed needed-- right then and there!

"My dumb luck!" Max said later.

It was about one in the morning when the ragged troupe hit the dark streets to go home. The water level had subsided and the hydroelectric utility had cordoned off or repaired downed wires. There was still no light in the homes and shops of Brackendale so upon arriving home, they all went straight to bed, exhausted but strangely happy.

* * *

By morning, the power was on and Robert Normal was brewing coffee and the TV news was on. Perry's older sister Gabrielle was at the breakfast table in her nightgown and robe, her honey hair loosely pinned on her head. The cat, whose fur was roughly the same color as Gabby's, was purring and sliding against her legs.

"Morning, Perry," Mr. Normal said in his usual cheerful tone. It was a mystery that Science could not explain: that a workaholic financial analyst with an accounting certification would wake up happy every day of the week.

"Morning," said Perry. He slumped into his chair and starting dumping cereal into a bowl, then sliced a banana on top, and filled the whole mixture with milk to the brim of the bowl. He did not even look up until his bowl was empty.

"Where *were* you yesterday?" Gabby said. "The news said that eleven counties were hit by severe weather and tornadoes destroyed entire subdivisions across the Ohio River Valley. I didn't realize that you were out in that mess! Were you with your friends?"

"Yeah, we volunteered to help the FEMA headquarters that they opened down on Athens Avenue. There were National Guards there; we got to ride around on a couple of missions. There was a schoolbus wiped out on County Road 10 when a cell tower blew down right on their bus. It was freaky! We had to get the kids out and into a special ambulance. Two had died, from what -- I don't know, so it was kinda creepy."

"They don't expect you to put your own life in danger in a rescue operation do they?" asked Mr. Normal, setting his coffee mug on the table as he sat down.

"Well, yes and no—they know we were trained and they know there's a risk and that's why they need a note from parents to acknowledge that they are aware that their child may be in a hazardous situation. Anyhow, we went to the community center later where lots of people without power had congregated. It was kind of fun, being there, helping them."

"You are a brave young man," Perry's mom Lisa said, breezing into the room. "Surely we can give you something more than cereal for breakfast!"

"Thanks, Mom. I am kinda hungry. It was an interesting experience, something unlike anything I ever did before. Makes you think about how dependent we are on each other and on the official agencies that are responsible for keeping things running."

The news announced a special bulletin warning residents of Ohio and Indiana of more rain and possible flooding in low-lying areas. They showed dramatic footage of homes and vehicles being engulfed by raging brown waters and swept violently downstream.

"Hundreds are missing at this hour, as casualties increase in local emergency rooms..."

Lives were lost but Perry felt strongly that their small contribution somehow helped their town and even the people of Upper New York State.

"Can you make some bacon please Mom," Perry said. "I think I'm going to need a holiday after this summer: FEMA boot camp and the strange coincidence of a local emergency right after we did our training. Like we were being prepared for that!"

"Your Father and I have no plans this year, not like last year in Florida when you got to do some scuba training. But your uncle has a vacation rental down in Redondo Beach and I can ask him if we can fly you down to Los Angeles for a week or so. Would you like that?"

Perry remembered his Mom's younger brother as the one who admitted seeing a UFO over Lake Ontario while camping a year or so ago.

"Sure, then I could maybe swing by NASA and see what's been going on!"

"Well don't get yourself into something weird again, Perry," his mom said. They were worried that the government would remember the kid who saw things in Space that he was not supposed to talk about, not publicly, anyway.

"No worries, Mom. I don't plan to get up to anything."

But Perry Normal knew that whether he was looking for them or not, weird things had a way of finding *him*. And it was still August, weeks before classes and school would pull him back to his studies.

Chapter Thirteen   Unstable Earth

The flight to LAX was over before Perry had time to adjust to the idea that he was in sunny California again. The contrast was made more vivid since he came from the ruins of a series of storms that had trashed the Great Lakes states.

'Like the difference between night and day' his Granddad used to say. Perry missed his Gramps and Nona. It was only months since the terrible crash -- but it seemed like years. He had not fully gotten over their deaths. He had not gotten over Renee's sudden exit either. This whole year so far had been a string of tragedies -- like Life had saved them all up and dumped them on him all at one time.

'Things can only get better, right?' Perry thought to himself.

Uncle Herman and Perry's two cousins were in the Dodge Caravan waving as he emerged from the terminal dragging his suitcase.

"How's things, buddy?" said Uncle Herman. He said 'buddy' to everybody like he was friends with the whole world.

"Hey, Uncle Herman. Hey, Sam, hey, Pete. You guys having a good time down here?"

"Totally!" said the two boys enthusiastically. "We wanna move here, but Dad says not before he retires --which will be in ten centuries!"

Perry enjoyed his male cousins. His sister Gabby was a few years older and she was—of course—a *girl*, which changed the rules of the game considerably. He couldn't tell her everything, he couldn't hang out with her: she was his sister. But these guys were mischievous and always had bizarre pranks up their sleeves so Perry could enjoy being a little bad while in their company.

For instance, Pete pulled out a BB-gun replica of a pistol that looked real enough to fool anyone. In a state where gun crimes and robberies were at an all-time high that was probably a stupid idea but that's how his uncle's family was: jokers, pranksters -- but good people who wouldn't hurt a fly.

This might be a fun week Perry was thinking.

But Perry could sometimes be wrong, too!

* * *

It was a very hot sultry day in the San Fernando Valley. The whole Greater Los Angeles area was sweltering in temperatures in the mid '90s and some days over one hundred degrees. Traffic was snarled from downtown to the I-5 interstate, and tempers were starting to fray in the traffic chaos as horns blared and people were yelling out the window in frustration. The highway had streamers of waves from the heat rising into the haze as Perry and his cousins were returning to their hotel near the beach where it was slightly cooler since the ocean here has a cold Pacific current that passes the California coast.

They had, in fact, just parked when the shaking began.

Just like that—everyone who felt they were broiled by the heat had a bigger concern: earthquake!

Every Californian is acutely aware of the faultlines that run up the coast from Mexico—San Andreas being the major one that was considered to be a permanent threat to cities like L.A. and San Francisco, but there were others just as deadly-- just not as famous.

The shaking tends to last only seconds, but its effect on every structure, every bridge and freeway, every bottle on the shelf of every kitchen and convenience store is quickly seen and felt.

The News Four broadcaster was already on it.

'Authorities are reporting a significant quake of about Magnitude 7 in the Los Angeles region. Damage reports are starting to flood in...'

Sirens began to wail and people were out in the streets, many panicking from collapsing ceilings in office buildings, falling shelves and light fixtures, computer screens crashing to the floor, and people fleeing the darkness inside, only to find debris and glass outside--on the sidewalks and roadways, cars honking and driving into one another in a vain attempt to flee. It was a scene from a disaster movie!

Perry, Sam and Pete were watching all this live, on television, yelling and pointing as the footage switched to a traffic helicopter, where the full extent of the quake could be seen. Smoke was rising from a dozen fires from broken gas lines, the freeway had fractured into several pieces that were not even connected anymore. The commentator said that local dams were in danger since large cracks in the concrete foundation walls were spurting fountains of water.

A police spokesman said *"Shelter in place, do not go outside at this time."* They didn't want thousands more in harm's way than they already had.

"Why don't we have earthquakes in the Great Lakes region, Perry?" Sam was curious and a bit shocked by what they had seen on TV.

"Different geology, Sam," said Perry. "Totally different kinds of rock. That rock is very old and does not move," he added.

"Maybe we should think about going home," Herman said. "This is not making for a nice holiday like we planned. Should've gone to Florida like your Mother said."

Herman scratched his head and fiddled with his moustache. He looked a bit uneasy.

"Can we get out of L.A. Dad?" Pete and Sam were firing questions at him, until their Mom came in the room. She had been at the outdoor market when the quake hit, and she was not in a good mood.

"What did I tell you, Herman? What did I say? California gets earthquakes and tsunamis and God-knows-what; and here we are. We should have gone to Tampa."

"Oh hi, Perry! Did you have a good trip out? Welcome to another disaster area."

"Hi Aunt Thelma. This is not what I expected. Is the Internet up?" Perry asked. "I can check the status of flights out." Perry saw that the airport was functioning and planes were leaving but inbound aircraft were being directed to San Diego Lindbergh airport temporarily. Perry was wondering if he would be flying out soon too--Aunt Thelma was ready to pack and skedaddle back home.

There was an email from Henry, asking if he was okay since the national news was covering the quake situation.

'Yeah, I'm good, Henry. Hardly felt it here. But my aunt and uncle probably will leave later today or tomorrow, so I don't have anywhere to stay. What's up with you?'

'I got an email, Perry, from one of the Cornell Physics grad students who works with Professor Wegener and he told me that there is a team already in L.A. who are following up on the quake in their study of West Coast seismology. Do you want me to forward the email to you? Maybe your folks will let you stay if you are with them.'

'Definitely! That would be awesome. Then I could stay out here a bit longer. I need a break after all that stuff from the storm. I can't get those kids from the schoolbus out of my head. Do you think I have PTSD or something?'

'Jeez, Perry, I don't think so. Then I would have it, too, right?'

'Yeah I guess so. I just feel tired Henry. I don't want to think about school or my friends --or emergencies of any kind. I'm kind of upset that I came all the way out here only to be in an earthquake. I mean, what are the odds?'

'Always happens to you, Perry. You're like a shit magnet. You can't escape it, man. It's your karma!'

'Thanks a lot, pal. I feel a lot better now. Let me follow up on this Cornell project and get back to you.'

'Sure, Perry. I'll say 'hi' to the gang for you. BTW Robert fell off his bike and broke his arm. He's in a cast and not happy about it. Talk soon!'

* * *

Professor Wegener had a crew of five physics and geology students who had funding to do research on the Pacific Coast related to volcanoes and earthquakes. It was just dumb luck that this seven-point-oh hit when it did. They had planned to start a week earlier but had headed out to the coast just the day before. Professor Wegener was reached on his cell.

"Of course I remember you, Perry Normal. You are one of us; you are a scientist to your bones. We would be delighted to have you aboard. We have arranged accommodation and transportation for four weeks. I can send your parents an itinerary. We are going to go up to some volcanic areas like Mt. Lassen and Mt. Shasta next week. My student Peter will give you directions to our hotel; I don't know if a taxi or bus can get through but I assume the city will rebound quickly. See you either tonight or tomorrow. Okay?"

Perry was blown away. *'This is perfect!'* he thought. *'This is the rainbow after the storm! This will give me the break I need by forcing me to be the scientist for a few weeks, instead of the reluctant hero who never asked for trouble but got it anyway.'*

"That's good dear," said Aunt Thelma. "Then you can stay longer. Are your parents okay with it?"

"They are fine so long as I report, like, twice a day. Dad gave me a credit card account of my own before I left so I won't have to worry about money or expense."

"Excellent," said his aunt.

"Can we have a credit card too Mom?" said Sam in a really whiny voice.

"Over my dead body!" said Aunt Thelma. "Now go and get packed; we are leaving in two hours."

Perry bid goodbye to his cousins, and his auntie and uncle, in the lobby of the hotel.

"Can I come visit you some other time? I wanted to spend more time, but..."

"Absolutely, Perry. Why don't you come camping with us on a long weekend this Fall? Something that we always do—it's a ritual," said Aunt Thelma.

"I will call you when I get back to school. Thanks for having me."

Perry gave her a hug, and punched both Sam and Pete in the shoulder playfully. He shook Uncle Herman's hand; Herman slipped him fifty bucks—'for snacks'.

* * *

The taxi took them to Los Angeles airport; Perry's taxi took him to a small hotel in Santa Monica, where the research team was holed up. He found them in the bar, having cool beverages and nachos.

"Perry!" Professor Wegener introduced him, remarking that Perry was a 'pioneer' in time travel and related matters.

"I just want to do good Science," Perry began. "Science can explain anything and everything --in my book. It's really what drives my curiosity."

Then he told them something even Professor Wegener did not know—he summarized his adventure at JPL and the bizarre follow-up by the Army sending a letter to his school. He wondered whether he should mention the Men In Black episode that came after.

"Do you guys know anything about MIBs?"

"Men in Black? I thought that was just Hollywood," said Nick, a Ph.D. student.

"Well, it has been reported numerous times by people who have had...ah...close encounters of the third kind."

"UFOs? Really? That happened to you?"

They were all leaning in to look at Perry and hear what he had to say.

"In a way, yes. Extraterrestrial contact. Nobody knows who they are or why MIBs appear. They have one thing in common: they intimidate the contactees, threaten them. Well, they came to see me two months after my JPL internship…". Perry told them every detail.

"That is so freaky," said Jennifer, a grad student in Geophysics at Cornell.

"I want to see a UFO," said Peter, who had invited Perry to try to join their little project.

"Hang out with a telescope, Peter," said Perry. "Trust me! You'll see a lot more than you might want to…out *there*, I mean." He looked up through the skylight as the first stars came out.

* * *

"We want to work with the USGS to analyze what triggered this quake and then we need to get into the field in the Cascade Range to see if there is increased activity in the chain of volcanoes we plan to study."

Professor Wegener was chairing a meeting in the conference room of the hotel. Perry noticed there were quite a few local students from UCLA and U Cal attending --as well as local media. Politicians were demanding answers. The governor was trying to restore calm in the City of Angels. Most of all— people wanted to know if the danger was over.

"Professor. Is the threat over?" the television reporter asked through a microphone.

"It is too soon to tell but in my view the energy that caused this has been spent and we should be able to go back to our daily routines."

Then during a flurry of questions from the audience, the Cornell team had a brief break and snuck off to Starbucks.

"Do you think this is the beginning of a period of seismic and volcanic activity?" Perry was speaking to his colleagues.

"That's what some experts think, Perry. There is evidence in general that the Earth's crust is moving more than usual, that massive forces deep underground are pushing magma to the surface. We see it in Italy, in Guatemala, in Indonesia, in Alaska."

"But this is California, one of America's jewels, and if there is no guarantee of safety for its residents, people are going to leave," Perry said.

"All we can do is monitor and measure ground displacement, steam and gas venting from mountains running up the coast. We don't want another Mt. St. Helen's!"

Nick murmured his agreement. Peter stared down at his latte, like it was going to erupt and spray hot liquid on him.

"Let's go back," Jennifer said. "I think the professor will be ready now."

The lights were down and the timeline for the research project was up on the screen. The reporters had all left to file reports, so only the team was present.

"Alright everyone. Let's look at the map. We've got a lot of ground to cover in three weeks. Working with us will be Wilbur Smith of the United States Geological Survey and G. Roy Long of the University of Washington who is an expert on the Cascade Mountains and their history."

The researchers on the project –including Perry -- split up, each with a particular task and each with highly technical equipment for measuring and inspecting and probing every square inch of ground that had been chosen for investigation.

Perry was with Nick and Jennifer that were reviewing historical eruptions with Dr. Long's well-known book as their bible; it had everything there was to know about West Coast volcanism.

Professor Wegener was speaking at the podium again.

"This quake occurred along the same fault -- and struck the same way -- as the 1996 Northridge Quake. Some of you will remember that one. Close to a billion dollars in damage.

What we aren't sure of is how it connects—or even *if* it does—with the volcanoes that are found in central and northern California. There is an urgent need to find out if these volcanoes are likely to wake up and if so—what the consequences will be.

We can see the destruction in Hawaii that has been occurring and that was predicted. But California has not had an eruption since 1917 at Lassen Peak. So we will need to take a road trip up there and see what is going on."

The word 'predicted' made a bang inside Perry's mind that reminded him that Renee had predicted all kinds of things, some of which seemed to be happening. Take the volcano in Hawaii!

She had never said anything about earthquakes, or anything else, in California. Strange to think that she was just nineteen hours drive north of where they were now, in Oregon. May as well be a million miles, thought Perry.

"So let's get up early tomorrow and get the gear loaded in the vans, get breakfast, and hit the road," the professor was saying.

* * *

Perry wished Henry was there to share the adventure. Volcanoes were Henry's big love in life. Perry thought about inviting him but there wasn't time now. All he could do is go back to his room and talk to him on Skype.

"You doing alright, Perry?" Henry looked geeky with his haircut really short.

"Yeah. We are going to drive up north to look at old volcanoes. I sure wish you were here, Henry. I have nobody my age to talk to. I am just tagging along. Who cut your hair?"

"It's my new look," said Henry. "I am a trained emergency responder. I'm even hoping to take shooting classes at the range. But I'm still too young, they say. But I trained on Army-issue firearms in the summer, I say. You don't qualify for a permit, they say. You can make an exception; what if I ask the Army lieutenant, who trained me, for a letter? I say. They are a pain in the ass, Perry."

"I totally get it, Henry. It's not fair if you already have the skills -- from the National Guard -- no less."

"Will you post some photos on your Facebook once in a while? So the rest of us can see what the hell you are up to?"

"Haha, sure Henry. I just don't use my account very much. But I promise I will post some pictures of the places I'll be going. I hear we may go to Mt. Shasta, which, as you know, is both an old shield volcano, and one of the most beautiful spots in the whole United States."

"That is so *cool*," Henry said. "And check out the whole Telos thing. You know...the legend of the Lemurian kings that have an underground city there? I know very little about it myself."

Henry continued, "I do know that if you live to be seventy years old, you have a one-in-four chance of experiencing an eruption in the Cascade Range. Isn't that incredible?"

"I hope it doesn't happen while I'm there," Perry said. "I'm still on holiday, and after the quake in L.A. I really don't need a volcano... lava flows... who knows what could happen? I do not want to be dead, or even near-dead, like Renee."

"What do you mean? I know she was in a coma, but..."

"I guess I never told you the whole story. Renee actually died on that ski hill. She was non-responsive when they got to her. Somewhere along the line, she...her heart started beating again, but she didn't come back to consciousness for weeks. I didn't know until she told me that she was dead, clinically dead. No pulse, no breathing, nada."

"How do people know if they are dead or not, if they're *dead*?"

"You got me, Henry. But at least 3-5% of Americans have had a Near-Death Experience; do the math—that's 17 million people, Henry. I'm sure many of them don't speak of ito r only tell their doctors or nurses what happened to them."

"Freaky. Like alien abductions—happens to lots of people but they cannot or will not tell. Well maybe there are people here in Brackendale that had a brush with Death during the storm. I should ask around maybe."

"You do that, Henry. It will take your mind off guns for a while. I'll let you know about Shasta, ok?"

"I'm looking forward to that, Perry. Wear clean underwear!"

"Huh? Oh yeah! Your mom always said '*wear clean underwear in case you are in an accident*'. Like it matters! You're going to shit your pants anyway! See ya Henry!"

CHAPTER FOURTEEN   SHASTA

The difference between Southern California and Northern California is one that is only apparent if you travel there. Both regions can be unbearably hot in summer, but the cool mountain air along the Cascades as you rise up through the forest has a smell—a taste—that invigorates the body and soul.

The unearthly beauty of Shasta can be seen for many miles and rises majestically from the pinon pine plateau that covers northeastern California. It is a sight not easily forgotten. There are old rolling mountains in New York, such as the Adirondacks, but nothing like a pristine peak shining brilliant white in the distance, lord of the horizon!

All of those on the team were under its spell immediately.

The small town of Mount Shasta is nestled at its base, 3600 feet above sea level, and charming in its unique way because of its unusual population of nature-lovers, New Agers, and just plain folks who have fled the crowded city.

"We have a camp further up the mountain -- thanks to the USGS. We can place seismometers, gas analyzers—all kinds of detectors because—remember—the peak is close to 15,000 feet and it is the peak that typically shows signs of disturbance or changes in its current dormant state."

Professor Wegener was laying out the plan for the week. The team had access to 4x4 vehicles and a bulldozer to remove topsoil and create clearings for geologists who would be coming later to establish a permanent presence on the 'volcano'—was what they called it.

Science was coming to visit Mt. Shasta to ask a few questions, like: 'Are you thinking of erupting anytime soon?' or 'Are you going to pose a danger to the citizens of California?'

* * *

What they weren't expecting was the local residents who were preparing a welcome party for them. Or maybe it should be called an 'unwelcome' party.

People with signs were circling outside the diner where the team was having breakfast. They were yelling something that Perry could not quite pick up, so he excused himself and stepped out into the bright sunlight.

'Save our mountain, save our Shasta!' they were chanting. But to whom?

Perry was not used to people marching in the street; this wasn't 1968, and this wasn't Washington or Memphis. This was pretty much nowhere. But here they were—chanting slogans as if the national media were right there to witness their struggle.

"Save our trees!" someone shouted at Perry. He was rescued by Peter who came out wiping coffee off his chin.

"We're not taking your trees. We are not loggers. We are scientists," he said.

"This is a sacred mountain. Do you know that?" hissed some middle-aged hippie woman wearing beads and rose quartz earrings and bracelets.

"We don't want negative energies here," she went on. "You people from the government all have negative vibes. You have evil intentions. The higher vibrations will force you off Shasta and bring peace to the inhabitants who honor her." Her bony finger pointed up at the summit, which was adorned in glaciers glinting in the August sun.

"Who is in charge here?" demanded Professor Wegener.

"The Lemurians," said a young girl with flowers woven into her fair hair. "They have come to lead us to the Higher Worlds and teach Mankind how to love spiritually and unselfishly."

Perry immediately thought back to the little Greek girl he met on Santorini; so innocent.

"Where do they live?" asked Perry, moving closer. "Who are Lemurians?"

"They came here thousands of years ago when their land Mu was swallowed by the sea. They have built a crystal city deep in the heart of our Shasta, and when the time is right, they will emerge and lead us to the New Earth," the girl said confidently.

"How do you know all this?" Nick said.

"Our spiritual guides have told many of us, and some people have channeled the Ascended Masters who protect this place as well. Do you know Count Saint Germain?"

"Ah, no," said Nick, "I don't. Does he live around here?"

"He is on the higher planes of existence but can manifest in Third Dimensional reality if the need arises."

"Well good for him," said Peter. "But we have work to do, so please recognize we mean no disrespect to you, or St. Germain, or the Lamour..."

"Lemurians."

"Right. Those guys. And we won't cut down any more trees that we have to, in order to build a camp. You are welcome to come check it out. Really."

Peter and the others loaded groceries from the adjoining market into one of the trucks, and the big diesel motor roared to life.

The crowd had settled down and soon disappeared in a cloud of dust as the team mounted the switchback road that carried them to the lower cone, called Shastina, which was formed in an eruption 7000 years ago.

"Shasta has a timetable you know," said Professor Wegener. Historically, if we look at the timeline of eruptions, they occur in either 200 or 600 years cycles, consistently over thousands of years."

"And where are we now, Professor, on that timeline?" Jennifer said.

"Funnily enough, it seems that we are in the two hundred year cycle and the last eruption was 1786."

"Sir? That is *over* two hundred years. Are you saying we are due anytime for another one?" Perry was asking what everyone was thinking.

"Precisely, Perry. Any day now. That is one reason why we are here. Perhaps that day will come in our lifetime," the professor said.

"Or maybe this month," muttered Nick, loud enough for Perry to hear.

* * *

They only had a few days to be physically on site on the volcano.

The team had a bewildering array of technology to put into place. Sensors, lasers, monitors, solar panels to power all the equipment that would stay behind. Perry was amazed and delighted to see how it all worked. Most of all, like everyone on the team, we was curious whether the volcano was likely to awaken anytime soon.

"We've got a FLIR camera trained on some fumaroles out there," said Peter.

Perry wanted to ask Henry what fumaroles were, since he was the volcano expert in Brackendale. There was terminology and geological history to learn here.

And somewhere in the back of his mind was what the girl had said about the lost city.

Why do people believe stuff like that? he wondered.

"Henry? What do you think of lost cities? We might have one right here in the volcano."

"Well, from what I know about volcanoes, the presence of large underground reservoirs of 3000 degree Fahrenheit magma might make that a little difficult!"

Henry went on.

"In the desert, sure—look at Egypt. Underwater? Absolutely! Look at the evidence for Atlantis we uncovered. But in the middle of a still-active volcano? Get outta town! Not happening!"

"The girl was not alone in her belief—there is a whole spiritual community in California that firmly asserts that Lemurians, and maybe extraterrestrials, inhabit the mountain somehow; how? I have no idea. But where there's smoke, there's fire, Henry."

"Speaking of: any detection by the instruments of hydrogen sulfide or nitrous oxide?"

"Oh Henry, you are just what I need to help me keep my feet on the ground! I think maybe the altitude is affecting me or maybe the New Agers are right and the high spiritual vibration of this place is zapping my brain.

Anyhow, so far, no reported gases. Hey! By the way: what is a fumarole and why are they watching them?"

"Fumaroles are small vents where sulfur and noxious gases produced by volcanoes escape. They are indicators of activity within the mountain and any change will be reflected in these vents. In Yellowstone the vents are steam geysers and are more obvious."

"Sure, I get it. What if we *do* find heightened activity, Henry? The professor said Mt. Shasta is on a timetable and is pretty predictable and we are due for an eruption!"

"Wow, that would be cool! Unless you are standing near the top—which you *are!*"

"Yeah, if this thing decides to wake up, I think the whole valley below has more to worry about than lost cities and aliens! I can send you the pictures I took of the hummocks from the last big lava flow—in fact, the town of Mt. Shasta is built on that. In any case, a pyroclastic flow or a mud flow would change the geography drastically."

"Hey, yeah Perry! You could be like Woody Harrelson in that supervolcano scene in the movie *2012*! Ka-boom! Wicked!"

"Haha, sure, and they would find my bones 10,000 years from now, fossilized, and buried in the ash and lava. Maybe I should have ID on me so they know who I was," Perry said.

"That would all be burned up, stupid. Maybe even your bones would be melted into the rock. And maybe we are getting silly here, cause the odds are very slim, my friend. What are you going to do after the project ends, what-- next Wednesday?"

"Not sure. I really wanted to get some beach time in California but that small matter of an earthquake kind of messed up my plans. Hey—I have to go. There's a commotion outside. Talk later, ok?"

"Do you have a gun?" said Henry with a hint of excitement.

"Hope I don't need one. Later."

* * *

They were back. The same crowd down in the village had managed to track them up to the camp, and were starting to mill about and hold up signs while some filmed the whole episode.

"We want you off the mountain!" said a burly bearded guy in a orange vest.

Peter and the professor came out of the trailer that served as camp office.

"We have authority to be here and to do our survey here," said Peter, who was bigger and more intimidating than the old professor who was now almost eighty.

"The Lemurians told us that you are not wanted. You are disturbing this holy place," said a woman with two long grey braids and cowboy boots.

"Can we speak directly to the...Lemurians?" said Jennifer, stepping up to face the crowd.

"They communicate telepathically and only to chosen messengers," said the woman with the braids.

"You are trying to show that our holy Mt. Shasta is some kind of geological menace, which is utter rubbish," said a man with glasses that had lens so thick you could have started a campfire with them.

"Off! Get off! Leave now!" The lumberjack and a handful of others looked like they might turn violent for a moment there.

Then Perry had a stroke of genius—and raw courage.

He stepped out in front, beside Jennifer and Peter and raised his hand.

"I have an important message for all of you. From St. Germain!"

The effect was instant! Not only did they hush down but the whole group sat on the ground with legs crossed, looking expectantly at Perry.

As if they knew what they had to do, Jennifer and Peter and the professor also dropped to the ground in a sort of yoga posture and Jennifer folded her hands in the traditional gesture of honor -- as if she knew something about what Perry was going to say was really special.

"Ascended Master Saint Germain, of the Violet Ray, and Protector of Mt. Shasta, has asked me to tell you what I am about to say."

Later, Perry would relate to Henry that this was one of the truly intense moments in his life! Because Perry had to make it up on the spot. But, as usual, he had done some homework.

"He says that this discord between us is not spiritual, and must stop. He says we are all Divine Children and that the Spirit of the Mountain welcomes our presence. He says the fact that scientists are checking the geological status of Mt. Shasta is one of the signs that the promised Golden Age is upon us. "

Perry saw out of the corner of his eye that some of the believers in the audience were weeping with joy, and raising their hands as if to receive some invisible blessing.

Perry's voice was like thunder and seemed to reverberate off the very stones around them.

"We must all unite our minds and hearts and souls in this sacred space and time! Attunement with the holy vibration of I AM and visualization of the violet ray entering our Third Eye will uplift not only this community of devotees but Humanity as a whole. So, I—Saint Germain of the Violet Ray—decree that peace and harmony shall prevail here—and on Planet Earth!

"I AM THAT I AM!" Perry seemed possessed. His voice rose in a shriek in his final utterance. The crowd went berserk with hugging and laughing and singing as if he had become their prophet in this timeless moment.

Jennifer was hugging the professor, who was too stunned to react, and Peter was laughing along with Nick and Harv -- although maybe not for the same reasons that the New Age crowd was laughing.

It made no difference! The whole camp – including the visitors -- was now on its feet, dancing and singing something like the Hare Krishna chant.

Soon enough the crowd dispersed to their trucks and old beat-up Chevys and went back the way they had come -- as a marvelous pink and violet sunset lit up the whole western sky.

"See, Perry? It's a sign!" said Jennifer with a smile.

"You see, Perry? I knew you were brought to us to help us on this project," said Professor Wegener. "I had a dream about you and you had a holy man in ochre robes beside you, if that makes sense."

"Really?" Everyone was amazed that the old professor would disclose something personal like that. Not his usual style.

The glorious colors of sunset gave way to deepest indigo, then black. Then a million stars emerged from the blackness so bright you could see your own shadow on the ground.

Soon, all were fast asleep, and the Spirit of the Mountain, too, slumbered in peace.

Upon returning from the long drive back to L.A., the team unpacked equipment and baggage in the lobby of the hotel, waiting for the van to take them to the airport.

By the time they were gone, Los Angeles was once more on its feet, still cleaning rubble and broken gas mains and water lines, but functional as a great city once more.

The mayor called it 'resilience'; the citizens called it a miracle.

The Dodgers were playing at Anaheim Stadium tonight against the Detroit Tigers and the parking lot was full by 5 pm. Life the way it is supposed to be!

Perry was at the counter arranging to stay over a couple of days, with his parents' blessings, so he could enjoy the legendary California summer just a little bit longer. He already had his timetable for school settled and classes were still a week off.

"Goodbye, Professor," said Perry, hugging the old Physics master tightly.

"Bye, Jennifer. Bye, you guys," he said, shaking hands all around, and waving as they pulled away.

Perry felt suddenly homesick, knowing they were flying back to Rochester and he wasn't.

Perry went to his room to shower and then went down for dinner in the Tex-Mex bistro attached to the lobby.

He went straight to bed afterwards, dog-tired from a long day, and a week of amazing experiences on the shining flanks of Mt. Shasta.

CHAPTER FIFTEEN   WHAT COULD HAPPEN?

Perry had his day planned out: go to the beach and relax. Play in the water, watch the California beach people play volleyball. Come home, and book a flight to Buffalo for the next day.

The sky was clear with a tinge of red on the high cloud. He switched on the television and KNBC News 4 had the weather forecast. 78 degrees, light winds from the southwest, UV Index moderate.

Munching toast from the hotel restaurant breakfast he brought back to his room, he flicked through the channels to see what is on at 8:30 am on the West Coast. He stopped at Channel 58 KLCS, the local learning network. A tarot card reader was in the middle of explaining what the Greater Arcana cards signify, particularly the scary ones like The Devil, Judgement, and Death.

Immediately he flashed back to the psychic Rosa and the tarot reading at the diner in late winter.

"The Devil does not necessarily refer to something evil, or that something really bad is going to happen," the reader on the TV was saying. "It's really a heads-up to be aware of our addictions to pleasure: food, sex, gambling, and yes—drugs and alcohol. It warns us to exercise some self-discipline."

Perry was lost in thought.

Rosa said that Death was not predicting someone would die, although Renee was very close to that cliff edge, hanging on to life. She explained that the Death card—and its position in the Tarot card spread—was talking about resurrection, about coming back from death. Maybe that's why Renee was so changed by her experience, her near-death experience. Like she had seen the 'other side' and knew something she could not find any way to express. So she withdrew from everyone, bit by bit. So really-- the reading was true!

"Now the Death card," explained the reader, "is often mistaken for a prediction that someone close to you is going to pass away, to die. That sometimes happens. But the Tarot is a teacher; it wants us to get the spiritual lesson in Life's experiences—both good, and bad."

Perry wiped his mouth and drank the orange juice from the takeout package.

"Death is an ending of some kind and often appears in a spread to signify that the Old has come to an end, its energy spent, so the New may now appear. Like the flower on a branch withers so that the fruit can come forth in that exact same place on the plant. So don't think of the Death card as an evil omen; far from it."

Perry turned it off. Time to think about sunlight and waves, not foreboding things.

He decided to wear his swimsuit under his shorts; that way he didn't have to look for a changeroom once he got to Huntington Beach. Towel, water bottle, wallet, room key. The front desk said there is a tourist shuttle that swings by Laguna, Huntington, all the way up to Venice beach, all for six bucks, and it stops right in front.

Perry slipped his RayBans on and slid into a window seat. Most of the passengers were older, tourist-types, with straw hats and smears of sunblock on their arms and legs.

It was 9:30 a.m. Another day in paradise; but this one belonged to Perry.

* * *

Perry started with the boardwalk that ran between the beach and the parking area. There were tables with umbrellas and hot dog stands, and espresso bars. Most of the customers looked like regulars who spent the lazy days of August right here, right on the Pacific Ocean, just hanging out. They dressed in any old way, with cutoff shorts and tank tops and all had sunburned noses and shoulders.

'Beachbums' his mother Lisa called them. Right now, Perry wanted very much to be a beachbum.

He pulled up a chair, put his iced tea and muffin in front of him and tapped the sand out of his sandals. A pretty young lady was seated at the next table and her eyes were as blue as blue could be. Perry looked at what she was looking at: it was a Tarot spread on the table being managed by an older lady in sunglasses wearing too much lipstick.

That's freaky! Perry was thinking. *I turn on the TV and there's a Tarot reader; I come to the beach, there's a Tarot reading in progress. Is there some kind of message here?*

The girl gasped, and put her hand across her open mouth.

Perry leaned over as carefully as he could without being obvious.

The sixth card—in the 'immediate future' position of the Celtic Cross spread—was Death. You could tell that card a mile away. It was black armor on a bony white skeleton riding its spectral mount.

The woman spoke in a soothing voice and the girl removed her hand but her expression did not change. She turned aside momentarily and her gaze caught Perry for an instant.

He wanted to hold her, comfort her, tell her that it doesn't mean what she thinks it means.

She broke her gaze and told the reader to go on. She knew—like everybody knows—that the cards have meaning collectively, as a whole picture, a summary of a moment in time—like a photograph. She wanted to see the rest of the cards.

But Perry did not and unobtrusively picked up his drink, silently moving on, shaking his head as if he were in a dream and should wake up now.

A sign caught his eye as he got out onto the sand at last.

NO LIFEGUARD ON DUTY

Perry realized that—yes, this was a beach-- and there were likely to be swimmers who were not strong and might get into trouble. His friend Rowan, at school, was a lifeguard at the local community pool. New York didn't have beaches, or surf, or much water other than the Finger Lakes, or Lake Ontario. All this was new for him.

A small group of surfers in wet suits were huddled near the shore, talking about something. Perry veered toward them, trying to eavesdrop. Perhaps they might have a tidbit of information that would be interesting. After all, they knew these waters; they were local kids.

"We could wait, or we could just go in," said a tall boy with a shock of blond hair.

The girl next to him said, "We should wait for the big surge they said on the news. That typhoon off Mexico is bringing a storm front and we might see some really bitchin' surf off here. They already have some of it in Oceanside. My friend there texted me. Look!"

They bent down to look at the images on the screen.

Perry drifted to a small dune where he parked his stuff.

Do I need a wetsuit? Is the water that cold?!

He folded his sunglasses and wallet into the towel, which he stuffed back into his pack.

Let's find out.

Last summer Perry had taken his scuba diving qualification in Florida -- where he was on vacation with his family and his best friend Henry. So waves and tides and oceans in general did not faze him.

He loved the smell and the freedom of being carried by the salty surging waves. It made you forget anything that was bothering you; you could just surrender to the power of the surf, kicking and splashing.

It was much colder than Floridao nce you were out in it. Cool currents came up from Ecuador, right up past the Baja, past San Diego, up to Mendocino. Hot sand, cool water. It was an odd combination but so far Perry was just content to thrash around in the shallows, just getting used to being in the sea again, like a sea turtle returning to its home.

* * *

He looked for the girl with the blue eyes at the table in the distance but she was gone.

Perry pulled for the deeper water, his arms and shoulders and chest working in unison, moving him further and further from the shore.

Treading water, he realized he was alone out here and the dark blue beneath his body was now probably a hundred feet deep.

Further still, he saw a pod of dolphins leap, throwing sparkling drops as they broke the surface, diving cleanly -- with no splash. Perry was glad he was not totally alone.

The swells were larger now. They lifted him way up, then dropped him down, like a teeter-totter, and he had to catch his breath before he hit the troughs.

The rip current was starting to pull him and he found himself kicking harder to stay within sight of the beach. He was starting to swallow water.

He had to get into the shore while he still had strength; this current was fighting him and he knew only one would win. He began to furiously drive his whole body to aim for shore.

The wave would lift, lift, and carry him forward.

The undertow would grasp his legs like invisible hands and pull, pull, and he could see he was not getting closer at all.

His arms pulled and his straight legs kicked hard as they could.

There was no one in sight—no surfers, no beachbums, no boats, no nothing --nothing but foam and spray and dark water, water that was becoming so cold his muscles... began... to stiffen... and no longer... obeyed his command to... pull... and kick... and pull...

Suddenly the sun burst into his mind and all the colors of the light. Perry was lifting out of his body as if he could float like a cloud; he *was* a cloud. The light enveloped him, infused him, became him.

Then he saw the tunnel. It was like, like a whirlpool, but it was dark inside as he went in. There was light way at the end of the dark and he moved toward it; it pulled him. It was a strange sensation.

Then The Bridge appeared --made of opalescent hues, ever-changing in pastel colors. *Where does that bridge lead?* Someone was speaking to him, someone familiar. That's all he could remember.

* * *

The noise was annoying. *Why is everybody talking in the middle of the night?*

Perry was in bed. The tube in his arm was annoying too. As he began to become aware of his surroundings, he realized it was, in fact, morning, and the bright sunlight shone on the floor of his room.

What room?

Then the nurse appeared out of nowhere and spoke to him.

"How are we doing this morning?"

Doing what? What have I been doing? Where is this?

Her fingers touched his wrist to feel the strength of his pulse.

"Are you feeling any pain?" the nurse asked.

"No," Perry said but his voice cracked, startling him.

"How many fingers am I holding up?"

"If you count the thumb as a finger...five," Perry replied.

"Good. Do you know where you are, Perry?"

"No, not really. I mean, in a hospital, I guess."

"You were brought in yesterday afternoon and have been unconscious until now."

"Who? How?" Perry had difficulty assembling his thoughts.

"You were rescued by some surfers who spotted you lying in shallow water about twenty yards offshore. You had a swimming accident and it looks like you drowned out there and were carried in by a strong wave."

"I remember a tunnel, and an arched bridge, and light...that's all I can remember."

"Why don't you just rest and we will have the doctor look in on you later? By the way, someone in the group found your wallet so we called your parents in New York. They are on their way to L.A."

"Thank you," Perry mumbled, although he wasn't sure who he should thank or what he was thanking them for. His head felt like it was packed with wet feathers. He slipped back into sleep as soon as she left.

He wanted to thank the man with the long hair who was with him, after the dolphins. He had tremendous warmth and love. Perry wanted to ask if he was Jesus but he was dressed like those monks in India in orange robes. He didn't look like the Jesus of Sunday School who had light skin and blue eyes.

Then he was swimming again, in the light and the colors flickering, like a strobe of alternating light and shadow, like what a ceiling fan makes on the wall when it's summer and it's hot in your room.

He was letting go again, like he did in the surf when the current took him under. Not deep down into darkness but into a radiant atmosphere in which he was weightless, like he had no body. Where he was free in every sense. Where he felt truly alive!

Chapter Sixteen   Truly Alive

"Perry? Can you hear me?" A man was speaking; he was sure it was a man.

He opened his eyes and shielded his face with his hand. *Who's this guy?*

"I am Doctor Raymond, Perry. I am responsible for your treatment here at St. Germain Hospital. We are keeping a close eye on you. I want you to make an effort to stay awake. Can you do that for me?"

Perry nodded. *Why does he want me to stay awake? I like sleeping, I prefer to sleep.*

"Ok, we are going to do some tests on you, so I want you to sit up for me. Then we are going to have an MRI done this afternoon and we should know more then."

A nurse came to the door and called the doctor out into the hall. He nodded and came back inside.

"Your Mom and Dad are here so we will give you a chance to catch up a bit later after we perform a couple of procedures. Can you lift your right leg? Left? Good."

And so they went through a diagnostic checklist to see if Perry was functioning normally. They peered into his eyes and had him answer simple questions like the ones his Second Grade teacher would do.

Soon they wheeled his gurney down a long hall into a darkened room where the scanner was kept. They lifted him onto a moving table that slid him into the magnetic core. It was a kind of dark tunnel and seeing that, Perry slipped into unconsciousness.

When he awakened, he was in his hospital room again, and the nurse was talking to him.

"Perry? Perry? Can you hear me? Can you open your eyes?"

Perry opened them. The nurse had a look of concern on her face. The doctor came in and spoke quietly to her.

"Perry? Can you sit up?" They pushed a button and the bed lifted him so he could sit.

"Do you feel that you could drink some juice? Are you ready to see your parents?"

Perry answered 'yes' to both those questions. He was feeling a bit better. He could stay awake.

"Can I get something to eat?"

"I think we can manage that," the doctor said. "No heavy food; maybe start with orange juice and cereal."

The nurse slipped out the door. When she returned, she had a tray.

And she also had two visitors with her.

"Perry!" Lisa Normal rushed to the bedside and threw her arms around her son.

"Hi, Mom!" Perry said, as if everything were perfectly normal, and he was in bed on a Sunday and she was waking him up to join the family downstairs.

"Perry! How do you feel, son?"

Robert Normal came and sat down in the chair they keep beside hospital beds for visitors.

"Pretty good, Dad," Perry said.

The nurse put the tray on a cart that allowed him to eat and talk to his parents at the same time.

"The doctor said the tests look good, Perry," his Mom said. "He said they can let you go home tomorrow if nothing further develops."

Perry wolfed down two poached eggs, two pieces of white toast, and a wedge of cantaloupe, like he wanted to set a world record for speed-eating a breakfast meal. Oh, and the juice, too. He even asked for another, and got it, and sucked that back as well.

"Sorry to be trouble, Mom," Perry said. Suddenly he was weeping, and his Mom lost it.

"You are never ever trouble, Perry! Do you understand that?" Tears were pouring down her face while she was dabbing a tissue on his face and stroking his cheek like she did when he was little, and got sick --when she cried and cried.

The nurse left the room as Perry and his parents celebrated the fact that Perry Normal was going to be okay, was going to go home, and everything was going to be alright again.

"You had a close call, son," said Robert. "How did you get yourself into that situation? You should have known there were risks. They've had shark attacks in these waters lately. Your mother and I were just shocked when the hospital called.

Oh, I'm not blaming you, Perry, I'm just blowing off steam. Gabby was hysterical, so we'd better give her a call tonight to say we'll be home soon."

"I wasn't paying enough attention to the situation, Dad. But things happen for a reason. I think this whole California episode is supposed to teach me something. I feel like I am a different person, somehow. But I am so glad to be going home to Brackendale."

* * *

"Are you *kidding* me?" said Charmaine. "Start at the beginning."

Perry and the diner gang were together, as always, sharing every moment, and Perry had them enthralled with his Shasta tale. He was holding back a bit on the Near-Death Experience at the beach.

"I couldn't believe they were hassling us about being on the mountain, #1, and #2 that they let me convince them to back off just like that. It was no different than me debating in school, only I had to be a bit larger than life. Anyway, it worked."

"Hey, Perry! Welcome back!" Robert and Max had just drifted in, having just heard the news about Perry returning home.

"Things are so boring here I thought about joining the service just to get away," Robert quipped. "You sharing your California tale? We wanna hear it too."

Robert ordered a ton of food, like always. Max was not as greedy, but he had a big appetite too.

"Do they think that Mt. Shasta is going to erupt soon?" said Margot.

"Well, if you mean by 'soon' --in the next hundred years, yeah, maybe," said Perry.

"Those people really believe there is an underground lost city and they aren't going to give up protecting what they think is...ah...sacred ground, I guess you would call it."

"I heard stories on Youtube about that," said Max.

"Yeah right! If you saw it on Youtube it *must* be true," Robert teased.

"Just saying. We don't know everything about the world, and there are many mysteries," said Max, turning his attention to his burger.

"You heard from Renee?" asked Charmaine.

"No, actually...no," Perry said.

"Something wrong, Perry?" said Rita.

Perry took a long breath.

"If I tell you something, promise you won't spread it around; it's kinda personal."

Robert paused, holding a fry in his hand, halfway to his mouth.

"Remember Renee was in the hospital? What she didn't tell us -- and I only found out later -- was that she had died out there in the snow."

"Died?" said Charmaine, Rita and Robert all at the same time.

"Yes. She was brought to the hospital in critical condition but they told her later that her vital signs were missing. Her heart had stopped. And during the time that her heart wasn't beating and she wasn't breathing she had an experience, an incredible experience."

"Tell!" said Rita, almost shouting.

"She floated out of her body up into a tunnel kind-of-thing. There was a light at the other end that was so bright and comforting, and a bridge of some kind, and she knew she was not in the place where her body was. She was herself, but not herself. I mean, she knew she had died and was perfectly at peace with that. Somehow she knew this was the gateway to Heaven and that she was at a point where she could choose to go over the bridge, or go back—to her body, her life on Earth."

"Well, why did she come back? I wouldn't come back," said Robert, matter-of-factly. "If someone gave me a choice to go to Heaven or come back to homework and school and the stupid stuff we have to do in our ordinary lives...seriously!"

"So why did she choose to come back?" Rita was insistent.

"She told me that someone was in the Light, someone loving, who seemed to know her and what she was going through in her life. And that someone said she had a choice, but that it was necessary for her to 'go back' and finish her lessons, or whatever, on Earth."

"You mean 'God'?" Max was really interested in where this conversation was going now. "She met God! That's awesome! See, Robert? I told you! God is really...real!"

Robert rolled his eyes, but could not say much in the face of such dramatic evidence. So he started on his second hamburger.

"Well, that is not the whole story," Perry said.

"What do you mean?" said Charmaine.

"I died in California. This experience happened to *me*. Just ten days ago."

The whole bunch of them reacted like there was a fire that just flared up under their seats.

"Whoaah, Perry!" Charmaine was in his face. "Are you telling us you dieda nd now you're back and somehow you know you died. Like...what is going on here? You'd better explain this in a way that your best friends can understand it."

As soon as she said 'best friends' Henry barged in the door, all out of breath.

"Hey, Perry. You didn't tell me you were back. What's everybody so excited about?"

"Shut up, Henry, he's about to tell us," said Charmaine.

Henry took the bench seat with Robert and Max and reached for some of Robert's fries.

"I was swimming and the water was cold but it was okay. I got a bit far from the beach without realizing that the tide and the waves were pulling me farther out. All of a sudden my body just locked up, I couldn't keep paddling. I went under and then I left my body."

"What does that mean?" said Robert.

"I just exited my body—through the top of my head and I floated up into the...well, I saw the tunnel, too, so I went up in it. It was sparkling and it pulled me up like a tornado or something. And when I emerged, there was a bridge over a river made of colors I've never seen before, and light, and music...like that song says '...sweet, fra-grant mea-dows of Dawn'.

I didn't know where I was, but I understand why Renee and people who have had an NDE might just want to stay there, in that heavenly place."

"But you came back—just like Renee! Did someone tell you to?" Rita said.

"Not really. I don't remember if they did. I did see some people, though. My Nona and my Grandpa were there but they looked like they were young again, but I couldn't get to them, they were just waving and smiling. And there were other people who I couldn't quite place but who seemed familiar. An Indian guru guy. He was so kind and I knew he would protect me or guide me. I don't know who he is but I have a feeling I will find out one day."

"Perry, really, how can you prove any of this scientifically?"

"The same way Renee did, Robert. The medical records show I was clinically dead when they hauled me out of the water. For how long? I don't know. They say that if you are dead, I mean brain-dead, for more than fourteen minutes, you will not recover. You'll either be dead-dead --or a vegetable for the rest of your miserable life."

"But you don't seem different to us," said Margot.

"I know something that very few people ever get to find out, my dear friends. I know that when we die, *we are not dead.* Not 'dead' in the sense that we don't exist anymore or have no awareness. I guess what this means is... that the concept of the 'soul' has some empirical validity."

"That's our Perry," said Charmaine. "That's the nerdy science genius we know and love!"

Everyone was chatting, and patting Perry on the back, and hugging him --and that was just fine with him. It was more than fine. It was as perfect a life as anyone could have. Without dying that is. There was plenty of time for that. Later. Much later.

THE END

Learn more about Perry Normal and his other adventures with his friends, by visiting author Mason Stone's blog.

https://perryisnormal.blogspot.ca

See his Author Profile and other books in paperback and Kindle editions at Amazon.com.

Order directly from the publisher Red Pine Publishing at: caveofwonders@gmail.com

www.ingramcontent.com/pod-product-compliance
Lightning Source LLC
Chambersburg PA
CBHW071602110726
47908CB00007B/2216